The German Officer's Boy

The German Officer's Boy

Harlan Greene

The University of Wisconsin Press
Terrace Books

The University of Wisconsin Press
1930 Monroe Street
Madison, Wisconsin 53711

www.wisc.edu/wisconsinpress/

3 Henrietta Street
London WC2E 8LU, England

1   3   5   4   2

Printed in the United States of America

Library of Congress Cataloging-in-Publication
Greene, Harlan.
The German officer's boy / Harlan Greene.
        p.   cm.
Includes bibliographical references.
ISBN 0-299-20810-9 (cloth: alk. paper)
1. Grynszpan, Herschel Feibel, 1921–ca. 1943—Fiction.
2. World War, 1939–1945—Germany—Fiction.
3. Hannover (Germany)—Fiction.   4. Refugees, Jewish—Fiction.
5. Jews—Germany—Fiction.   6. Trials (Murder)—Fiction.
7. Paris (France)—Fiction.   8. Assassins—Fiction.   I. Title.
PS3557.R3799G47   2005
813′.54—dc22   2004023301

Terrace Books, a division of the University of Wisconsin Press,
takes its name from the Memorial Union Terrace, located at
the University of Wisconsin–Madison. Since its inception in 1907,
the Wisconsin Union has provided a venue for students, faculty,
staff, and alumni to debate art, music, politics, and the issues of the day.
It is a place where theater, music, drama, dance, outdoor activities, and
major speakers are made available to the campus and the community.
To learn more about the Union, visit www.union.wisc.edu.

For

JONATHAN RAY

you raise me up

Prologue

On 28 March 1921 Herschel Grynszpan was born into an impoverished Polish family. Seventeen years later Nazi Germany unleashed a wave of horror on the world, blaming him. Since then, scholars, historians, apologists, and zealots have debated that boy and his actions.

What follows is premised on the contradictory statements made by Herschel himself. Much is fact and much is fiction. While this may be inevitable in the telling of anyone's life, it seems all the more so in the case of Herschel Grynszpan's.

***

In memory of my mother,
REGINA MIEDZYRZECKI KAWER GREENE,
who survived her generation's holocaust,

and my beloved,
OLIN BRADFORD JOLLEY,
who did not.

The German Officer's Boy

Herschel did not come to the world's attention until that unusually warm day—8 November 1938—when he walked into the German embassy in Paris.

He had been about to turn back when, at nine o'clock, nearby bells rang and the embassy gates swung open.

"I have secrets," he gasped to the others in line behind him as he was pushed in. He patted his coat pocket; something, a piece of paper or photograph, peeked over it. "I need to tell somebody," he said when a uniformed man asked him what he wanted.

"The ambassador?" The gatekeeper queried.

"Yes."

Ambassador Welcheck was out, and his assistant was not seeing anyone. Would he settle for the third secretary?

"I guess so."

The porter Nagorka was called to show him the way.

"Come," the old man said in German, motioning for Herschel to follow.

"A strange one," he thought, looking back and taking in the teenager's eyes—dark, unfocused, unearthly. His mouth was large, sensual, and grim. He squirmed and looked about uneasily—as if it hurt even to think. But these days, with talk of war, and couriers going back and forth, peculiar things like this were occurring. Nagorka pointed to a high formal door at the end of the marble hall. "Knock," he motioned, "and go in." The boy looked back reluctantly. His hands shook; his lips were moving.

Nagorka sat. After the boy knocked, the old man reached for a newspaper. He read and, despite himself, listened. In the room he heard a shout. Of joy? recognition? He read further. Suddenly, he was hurled from his seat; it was like an earthquake—he had been in one years before, in Turkey. He flung the paper down and ran, pushing the door open, ready to shout, but stopped when he saw the blood on the carpet and the pale blond man thrashing on the floor.

And then there was the boy. Never before had Nagorka seen such an expression. The young man looked up, distraught and horrified from beneath his tousled hair and dark brows, his eyes circles of fear. The gun fell from his hand.

"I did not mean it," Herschel cried, pointing to the man with blood spurting from his mouth, like lipstick gone crazy. "Help him!"

Later, the attorneys Szwarc and Vessine-Larue would tell anyone who'd listen how shabbily they were treated by that wretch, Herschel Grynszpan.

Szwarc would always begin with how busy they had been the morning that Herschel's uncle came in. "My partner"—that was Vessine-Larue—"and I were conferring with a client," he'd tell anyone who would listen.

In fact, when he heard the knock, Szwarc was complaining and fiddling with the knob of the new radio set, trying to get the details of the attack at the German embassy.

"Who is it?" he had called out.

No one answered.

So Vessine-Larue shouted, "Come in."

A dark, sharp-faced man with the look of someone hunted peeked in.

Solomon Grynszpan looked back and forth from Vessine-Larue—who was tall and portly, had frizzy orange hair, and was pale and perspiring—to Szwarc—an intense man with a thick black moustache threaded with gray who was picking bits of tobacco from his lip.

"What do you want?" Szwarc asked, turning down the volume on the radio.

"That!" The man nodded at the glowing dial. "Herschel. My nephew."

Szwarc shot up from his seat, smoothing back his thick unruly hair and putting out his cigarette.

"We were busy, but I fit him right in," Szwarc later would tell those who were interested in such a piece of history.

The visitor nodded and walked tentatively into the office; a queasy look crossed his face. "My name is Grynszpan. They say Herschel shot someone. And Abraham and Chawa—that's my brother and his wife—they're responsible for Herschel—have been arrested. The police . . ." He clutched his hands together. "He's a horrible boy. I never liked him; from the start I wanted to send him back to Germany!"

Szwarc nodded and reached for Grynszpan's hand. "Bring our friend something to drink."

A moment later Grynszpan took the cup of dark tea that Vessine-Larue held out to him.

"My wife has cups like these."

Szwarc nodded. "Drink. My partner and I need to speak."

He led Vessine-Larue into a small messy room. Szwarc barely managed to shut the thin varnished door before exclaiming, "Did you hear?" Trying to suppress his smile, he hit his forehead with the heel of his hand.

The orange-haired man danced a jig. "On the radio! An international incident. The German embassy!"

Szwarc cracked the door. "And he wants me!" He rolled down his sleeves, straightened his green and gold tie. "Where's my jacket?" He slipped it on and darted out.

"My associate and I will take the case."

Solomon Grynszpan rose, but Szwarc held out his hand. "Not so quickly."

Grynszpan cringed.

"You must not," Szwarc said, holding up a nicotine-stained finger, "speak to another soul about this; you have to promise you'll consult no other attorney."

Grynszpan nodded. Szwarc winked at Vessine-Larue. "It's most important."

"All right."

"He picked us, and agreed to our terms right away—which were generous," the attorneys would later learn to say. "But within a day he'd break his word, already be speaking to another attorney."

Szwarc had the confused man by the elbow and was steering him to the street. "Now . . . your nephew?"

"Yes. He's just a boy, really. And lazy! Never worked a day since coming here; we wanted to help, take in one of our brother's sons—save him from what's happening over there, but . . ." Vessine-Larue closed the door and followed Szwarc and Grynszpan down the dark stairs and into the warm sunny street.

"We don't agree with what he did; we're law-abiding people."

Vessine-Larue turned left. Szwarc handed the sweating dark Grynszpan into a taxi. The lawyer waved as if to his best friend. "Don't worry; we'll take care of everything."

7

Then he motioned for Vessine-Larue as he hailed another cab.

Ten minutes later the two lawyers got out in front of the police prefecture. Szwarc leaped out of the taxicab, and Vessine-Larue dug in his coat pockets for money. He wiped his forehead as he made his way up granite steps and through a series of blond beveled glass doors. Yesterday had been drizzly and cool; today was almost sultry. Police officers in rolled-up shirt sleeves looked up from the tables they were leaning over.

"We're the boy's attorneys." Szwarc thumped his chest, and the shirt-sleeved men raised their eyebrows. These lawyers were not to be believed; their usual clients were rent boys, petty embezzlers, thieves.

"They knew we were not to be meddled with and took us to Herschel's cell immediately."

He was certainly well dressed—in a pin-striped suit, cheap but neat. (They would approve of and clip the photographs of their client that appeared in the world's newspapers the next morning. They show Herschel Grynszpan as small, only an inch or two above five feet, underfed, and hardly the seventeen years his passport decreed.) His teeth were small with spaces between them, which made him look greedy. Except for his very black hair, he had no resemblance to his uncle Solomon that his lawyers could see.

When they entered, the boy looked up revealing serious, smudged eyes and droopy baby cheeks. He tossed back the jet diagonal of bangs as he tried to light a cigarette, but his hands shook, fumbling the match. "Ye-es!?" he cried, exhaling, voice cracking, the eerie whites of his eyes too much in evidence. "What's happening? How is he?"

"Who?" They could smell his animal panic.

"At the embassy, the man . . . this morning. How is he?" He spat his words out in a rush as if his head were pounding and each sentence was a beat of misery.

Szwarc looked at Vessine-Larue as he stepped forward, bowed, and clicked his heels. "We'll find out. Your uncle, our very good friend, engaged us."

The boy tried to nod, speak, but two other large uniformed men entered just then.

(Everyone, it seemed, wanted Herschel Grynszpan.)

"Who are they? What do they want?" the boy shrieked, as if his nerves were disintegrating.

They showed papers. Szwarc stepped back.

The guards reached for Herschel. "Where are they taking me?"

"Do not worry."

The guards' faces were as impassive as clocks. They grabbed Herschel under his arms, whirled him around, and led him out the door.

The halls twisted and turned. Ceiling lights burned with a dry electric clarity. Herschel felt faint, weighing

9

more and more as he descended to basements and cellars. Surely this was what the dead must feel in cemeteries. The wide hall ended in a door. The guard on his right knocked with his knuckles and then let the boy go. He fell forward into the office as its door opened.

A short rotund man with a shining bald head and round tortoiseshell glasses sat behind a blond desk. The man opened his palm, bidding Herschel to take a seat.

He collapsed into it; he could hardly breathe.

"You'll be charged, not as an adult, seeing you are just seventeen," the man was saying in French.

"Go slow, please," Herschel cried, raising his arm. "I speak German."

And the man obliged.

"In just a few minutes we will transfer you to Fresnes; it's a quite modern prison, brand new, just opened. You'll like it, as it uses the most novel of theories; it's for the young like you."

The man looked up.

"Can you write?"

Herschel nodded.

"Good. They'll want you to write down the story of yourself; they need to know what you believe, your dreams. It's part of their theory, to understand and explain you to society."

He handed the boy a book stamped with the words *Fresnes Inmate Diary* on the cover.

Herschel dropped the book. It sounded like a gunshot. He and the man both jumped.

"Oh, dear."

Only part of Herschel Grynszpan's diary would survive the war, and exist, in transcript, in London's Weiner Library.

Assignment: Use this book to tell about yourself. Put down everything relevant to your case and how you got here.

The Young Offenders Division
Fresnes Prison

This is my story. I tell it now—not because they make me, but because I have to. The world has to know what I did for my family—that's why I went to the embassy.

His family. What a joke.

Each morning Mama had followed him and Solly to the door. But he knew she had eyes only for Solly. "Be careful," she called out to her handsome son, as half-blind Berta peeked around the edge of the door.

"You know Mama loves you too," Solly always told him.

Solly and I went out every day. I, we, were all Polish, though we did not live there. "Any place is better than Poland," Papa said. There was no work, no food; the Poles hated us Jews, spit at us on the street. All of Papa's family had left long before—for France, and so we, Mama and Papa, Berta my sister, Solly and I, got to Germany. But we did not have papers. That's why they all were sent back, why I had to go to the embassy.

With more and more Jews arriving from Poland every day, we always went out to find work and see if we could find out anything about Mama's family.

The market, right across from our apartment, was dirty, but no one noticed and no one noticed me.

But everyone noticed Solly. He had dark glossy hair, blue eyes, dark brows, a narrow nose, and hollow cheeks. Everyone looked his way, men and women, Jew and Aryan. Solly was so handsome that it was shocking.

Farmers' wives sat at rough wooden tables that were painted green and piled high with potatoes, apples, and beets. Solly approached a gray-faced crone with sore gums and stumps of teeth.

He smiled, and she smiled back and reached for a pile of small green apples. "For you, good-looking!" she cried, tossing him one.

Solly caught it.

"Thanks!"

"Now you have to kiss me!"

"Later!"

She opened her mouth and licked her gums, collapsing her face. Solly whispered, "Disgusting," as he grinned at her. Still smiling, he grabbed another apple. Turning away, he polished it on his shirt. "Here."

"Thank you," Herschel mouthed, biting into the tart pungent fruit and almost crying.

Sometimes we had to steal. It got bad. We were hungry. But I always found something—if not for me, then my family.

Peddlers haggled and swore, pickpockets moved silently as cats, men in uniform cursed. By the stinking urinals three or four boys always lounged, grinning, and wiping their noses on their sleeves. When they saw Herschel, they nudged each other and laughed. They rose up on their haunches, put their hands to their mouths, and made sucking noises.

One day after Solly and I had split up, and I was alone, a group of boys who could tell I was a Jew—attacked me.

As Solly and Herschel passed the boys, Solly frowned, jerking his brother past the taunting group.

"I didn't want to! They forced me!"

Solly twisted his mouth. "Don't lie."

But Herschel had to lie; he had to make right what he had done at the embassy that morning, could not tell his family's sad, true, and demeaning story.

That day when I was alone, I was attacked. Papa said I must have provoked them. But I didn't. I swear. I did nothing. They could just tell who I was by looking at me.

But how? He wondered. Did he emit some scent or essence? Some people could spot Jews who were trying to pass. Could they tell who was what with other things too?

As he walked by, the boys got up. One stepped out from the wall that they had been leaning on and swaggered in front of Herschel.

His challenger was fair, with slanted Slavic eyes; he smiled and rolled on his heels like a sailor. "Want something to eat?"

"Yes!"

"So. Come on, then."

The boys parted to let Herschel slide past a plump redheaded boy who had his hands stuffed in his pockets.

"Here," a blond fellow said, looking back to make sure that Herschel was following the Slav. The blond exuded the scent of unwashed flesh, and underwear worn too long, but Herschel followed, moistening his lips, finding it hard to breathe. The blond boy's fierce blue eyes and the down on his arms appealed.

As they passed a shed, Herschel turned and saw a brick wall. The blond fellow had his jacket off and his pants down. His flesh bobbed, hairy and pink.

"Kiss it," the blond boy said in a husky voice as he reached out and grabbed Herschel's wrist.

Herschel shook his head but fell to his knees.

"It's kosher," the blond boy laughed, and his friends closed in a circle around him.

"I would have run!" he cried to Solly later. He would have too. "But that boy pulled—like a priest." In Poland the priests grabbed at you in the street and made you kiss the figure on the cross that they were bearing.

"Your Lord! Kiss it!"

"He made me!"

They attacked me in an alley. They saw I was a Jew, but Solly saw them. Solly saved me.

Herschel had a glimpse of his brother leaping over the table, teeth clenched, fists flailing. "No!" Solly screamed. "Herschel. Stop it! What are you doing?"

"Catch them," the Slav called. It brought the others to their feet.

"Catch them."

We got away; we escaped, running, with them following.

"Wipe yourself off," Solly cried, disgusted, dragging Herschel by the arm.

"It wasn't what you think!" Herschel ran along, pulling his pants up, tripping, everyone laughing. "They tricked me!"

But Solly shouted, "Don't lie. I saw what you were doing. You can't trust anyone, Herschel. Only family!"

With men it was disgusting. But sometimes men waited for Solly in the market, and it meant that he always had spending money. "Love," Mama said, shaping her mouth like spitting, "is not true." She said it was all a lie. "It means nothing!" she'd cry after she and Papa argued. Every time Herschel and Solly passed the boys after that, they laughed and snickered at Herschel, but they always looked gravely at Solly.

Every day Solly and Herschel went out looking; every day they went to find a new group of refugees. They milled around like pigeons. "Anybody from Novo Radomsk?" Solly would ask, trying to get information about Mama's family.

That morning he found a group of newly arrived Jews. It was just before Passover, and the men had gone off to pray or find work; the women—wives—sat huddled on their suitcases, clutching scarves about their wigged heads and staring at their feet. Solly approached and asked in Yiddish if they knew of the Silberberg family. Scared and sullen, they would not speak.

"I'm talking to you. Please answer me!"

One bruised woman started to cry. Herschel looked away, ashamed. He had never suffered. Everyone protected him. Protecting Herschel gave Solly something to strive for. Berta said it was the only thing she could do for a child, since she had no dowry, was blind in one eye, and would probably never marry.

"A daughter should help the father," Papa always told her when he found her caring for Herschel, saving him a scrap, singing in his ear, or rubbing his temples when his stomach hurt or his head ached. "Your highness," he spat at Herschel then. "You don't know suffering."

Herschel thought that anyone could tell how pampered he was just by looking at him. As they stood in front of the refugees, a desire to suffer rose in Herschel like a snake twisting in his bowels. If they heard a stranger's cry in the night, Mama would put her hand to her mouth. Berta would jump. And Solly would talk fast about Sophie, their sister killed by a crowd throwing bricks.

But Herschel, the youngest, had been spared from suffering, kept like a kitten in a drawer, as if he were not old enough, or suffering was too good for him, too dear. "The boy's been through a lot; he's important," he wanted to hear folks say one day when they did not know he was listening.

He watched Solly hold an apple out to the Jews. A young boy in the crowd lifted up famished eyes as if he didn't know an apple was something to eat. But then a girl in a dirty dress, who had lank hair and dark rings under her eyes, snatched it away and viciously bit it. As its juices slid down her chin, she glared at Herschel.

"Get out of the way," a woman in a wig, a rich Jewess

with a collar of mink, said, pushing through. The crowd of refugees melted back like fog, but Solly stuck out his chin and held out his hand to the woman.

"For Passover; for matzo," Solly cried. "For charity, another Jew! They're poor; they're from Poland!"

"Go away!" the woman cried, pushing at Solly, her fingers flashing with rings. "You Polish Jews are making it rough for us here." The woman looked disgusted. "Let me alone," she cried, pushing past Solly.

"Bitch," Solly called after her. "Your husband would do it with a sheep instead of you."

Herschel blushed.

I loved my family. I was sad when I had to leave.

It had started that day, the first of Passover. That was when it came together, in his own mind, at least. After scrounging in the market, Solly, his face pale and more ethereal now for its incipient blue shadow of beard, turned to Herschel and said, "We have to go."

They backtracked through the butcher's area, where blood ran down the drains in the middle of the brick street. At the door to their building they took deep gulps of air and held their breath, as if under water. They climbed past the trash and filth; holding hands, they broke into the apartment, gasping for air, so it sounded like they were almost laughing—except you could not laugh here.

The room, with darkness scowling in the corners,

was a bit warmer, at least. Solly shut the door. "Anyone here?"

Berta darted out from behind the blanket stretched along a string that walled off the corner that Mama and Papa's bed was in. Her bad skin and her one milky blind eye made Herschel wince; he looked instead at the rich cascades of her thick dark hair. He tried a half smile and she smiled back.

"Look at these." She turned to Mama's antique blue goblets, which were lying flat on the bed, laid out like rigid bodies.

"Where is she?" Solly asked, squeezing her shoulders gently before going over to warm his fingers.

"Down in the kitchen." Berta picked up a glass, blew, and made her breath appear on it. They were cobalt with knobby stems and gashed designs that looked like moons and stars etched into the blue. As she lifted one higher, the cuts in the crystal flashed clear.

"Be careful!" Mama called, as she bundled in from the hall. "Take care of nice things!"

Berta put her hands at her sides, watching Mama hold out her bony fingers; as Mama spied Solly, her cross look melted and her face gleamed like old silver. The tension across her sharp wide nose and high cheeks released. She took off the apron that she had put on over her faded mauve dress and stroked Solly's forehead.

"Darling."

Berta and Herschel watched Mama draw Solly to her cheek. Berta looked at Herschel and put a finger to her lips. She licked her fingertip and rubbed it around the rim of a goblet. Herschel smiled as the crystal sang.

And Berta smiled too. "You should be happy more often!"

Herschel's head snapped back. No, he had to be sad. Someone had to make it up to Mama for leaving her rich family and for marrying Papa.

He jumped when the door pushed open again, dragging across the floor in an arc. Papa came in and Herschel tried to look busy.

"What is it you are doing?" his father demanded.

"I'm helping set the table!"

"Pah!" Sendel Grynszpan looked disagreeable, with his red face, no eyebrows, a broad nose, wide wet mouth, and curly dark hair. His eyes, small curved slits, were vengeful, angry.

He blew on his hands. "Rifkah! What you got to eat?"

Darting back from the alcove, Mama put her apron back on, tying it behind her. "The master wants a meal!"

Sendel barked, "What are you saying?"

"Nothing!" she rolled her eyes, which flashed as blue as the goblets. "Quick," she said to Solly, "help me."

But Herschel leaped forward. "I will!"

"All right!"

Heady with happiness, Herschel followed her out to the dark smelly hall, down the unlit stairs into the low basement kitchen full of happy talk and laughter.

"Look who's here."

"The lady Grynszpan."

Laughing.

Mama brushed by, nose tilted up, treating the other women, working on their meals, like servants. Herschel tried not to catch their eyes; they looked like demons in the steam boiling up from the stoves.

"If she's so grand why'd she marry that Sendel Grynszpan?"

All the women, some with their holiday dresses on, clucked their tongues and wrinkled their noses at the greasy soup.

"Disgusting."

Mama hoisted the pot. "Get the door, Herschel!"

He did, knowing how Papa would warn, "You got to be nice to people, Rifkah; you're why no one respects me here."

Herschel looked back at the women through the steam and wished that they would accept his family. As he followed his mother into the darkness, he heard a woman say, loud enough for all, including Rifkah, to hear. "I wonder, since it's a holiday, if there'll be peace."

"I doubt it."

"Like dogs, they're always fighting."

We were hated by everyone in the building; they were mean; they were ugly. For no reason. They tapped their feet on the floor when we made noise, or hit the walls—"Polish Jews," they said. "Don't know how to behave here." As if Germany was the best country. They were jealous of us, how much better our manners were, how we did not stoop to their chatter.

At the seder Sendel led the chanting; Berta, who could not read the Hebrew, squinted at the tattered page of her Haggadah, smiling as Herschel showed her the place. Mama looked from the blue glass goblets to Solly. They spilled a drop of wine for each of the ten plagues that God brought on the Egyptians to free the Jews. Mama told how glorious the holidays used to be, how many guests they had back in Poland, in her family. Her father was a rabbi; they had a tallis factory. Herschel imagined all of them around the grand table, with God and the angels in attendance, the Egyptians reaching and screaming as the water rushed in, drowning Pharaoh's army. He smiled, thinking of it, smelling the food that Berta and Mama were bringing to the table. The candles gleamed. Conversation stopped as they all turned to their meal.

Herschel put his fork down when he heard the growling. Sendel pointed at the small gristly piece of meat on his plate and then at the thick joint with golden skin and gravy on Solly's. "Rifkah," he growled, "you're wanting a beating."

"Please, Papa, take mine," Berta offered, pushing her plate forward, her forehead creased. "I'm not hungry."

Solly stopped eating too. He was pushing his plate forward, but Mama extended her arm. "Make more money and I'll give you more to eat!"

My parents loved one another. They never argued about anything.

Papa grunted, and Mama laughed in satisfaction. She turned back to speak to Solly. Suddenly Papa picked up his cobalt blue wine glass with the white crystal stars across it. The red wine spilled across the moon-white cloth.

"My grandmother's," Mama screamed, reaching to dab at the stain with her napkin. "Put it down," she snapped at Sendel. Herschel held his breath as he watched. Papa enjoyed her nervousness. "An antique," Papa said, turning the glass in the light, "from the grand family." He drained the last bit of wine and smiled, showing dark teeth. He hurled the glass against the gray plaster wall and it exploded. Laughing, he smiled. His face was red, his eyes squinty.

"What do you think of that?"

"Wonderful!" Mama gasped, applauding. Color rose in her cheeks as if a force had exploded in her too, and she stood up. "What a man!" Papa leaped up too.

Mama's face got even brighter. "Idiot!" She slapped Sendel.

Papa just picked up another glass, Berta's—and she jumped, thinking he was grabbing at her. He slammed it against the wall.

"Idiot! Fool!" Mama screamed. "Destroy it all. Before we starve! Who else would be stupid enough to

24

bring us to Germany? Your brothers got to France at least!"

Papa's smile soured. "Right," he said tensely. "Keep it up, Rifkah."

And she did, raising her voice, in pitch and frenzy. His face darkened as she continued, "Do you know why no one in this building likes you!? Because they know it's I who keeps the family—me!"

A strangled gasp escaped from Papa as he reached for her and slapped. He screamed, "Bitch! I'll show you." She went limp, he tore at her dress, and she cried out, "What a man!"

Herschel watched hungrily.

But Berta called out, "No!" while Solly tried to shield his brother and sister from what was happening. But Mama was pulling at her own clothes, ripping them off, showing the old slip underneath. Solly yanked Hershel up by his arm, away from the table. Berta was up too.

"Let's get out of here."

I loved my family. They loved me.
He was in tears.

Berta was crying as they ran out into the hallway. Going down the steps, their feet hit the wood so loudly that the sound was shocking. They made sounds— they must be real.

All along the halls slots of light seeped under doors,

underlining the darkness. Other families were at their seders; Herschel half expected to see blood painted on doorposts, to show that they were good Jews and that the Angel of Death should pass over them. People shouted, "Be quiet, have respect, please!"

Suddenly, they were outside, beyond the stench that oppressed their senses; they were free and came to a standstill in the deserted streets. In the market there was only moonlight, a rising tide of light. A newspaper rose up like a bird beating its wings. Herschel saw Berta's shawl unfurl in the shadows. He shivered, as if it were an angel.

"I'm Moses," Solly cried, raising his arm.

"And I'm Miriam." Berta danced with her arms up, and all the shadows spun. The moon rose higher as she led them down the street. They went after her, turning here and then there, taking the roads that turned to dirt as they reached the outskirts of town. As if by law, buildings stopped abruptly. And the Grynszpan children stopped too. The land stretched vast and endless.

"Which way?" Berta asked.

Solly answered happily, "Let's go exploring."

"For forty years?"

And Herschel laughed.

Beyond fences and low barnlike buildings, cows lowed, and nearby a night bird flapped its wings. Nothing rose on the horizon but cottages, haystacks, and trees. The cold bit. Mesmerized by the unearthly beauty of the moon, and its ability to change things,

Herschel stopped to watch it. (What do you see, they asked, and he could not answer, not exactly; it was more of a feeling. It was like dust but also like dreams, wistful, silvery sad, and longing.) If he could play the piano, he would; the moon pulled out a yearning, like music snatched from wandering fingers on black-and-white keys.

And it was all black-and-white out here—but reversed, like a photographic negative. Berta and Solly walked on as Herschel stared at the moon, feeling it pour down its blessings. But then, when he saw that he was alone, he ran to them. They had plopped down near an abandoned tractor. Close by was one skeletal tree. A few crystals of ice glittered in the moonlight. Berta unwound her shawl and pulled Herschel close. She hugged him.

For a long while no one said a thing. But they all knew what each was thinking.

Solly pulled a piece of paper from his shirt pocket and held it up. He showed them his visa for France.

Berta touched it as if it crackled with magic or static electricity.

"Can we go with you?" Herschel asked.

"Certainly."

We had our plan. We knew if we got into France, it would be better for all of us. Papa had two brothers in Paris. They said they could use someone in their business, so they sent the paperwork for Solly. Once he got over, he'd work and send money for the rest of us—me first, then Berta, and then our parents. We would all be together again—so when on Passover, the visa came, it was as if Moses himself had come for us to take us to the promised land.

They looked at the piece of paper as one would an ember from which a fire might spring.

The air grew colder, more still. More and more stars popped out.

"Can you see them?" Herschel asked Berta.

She pulled back her hair, revealing her sightless eye, blank as a statue's, in the moonlight. She shook her head. "What are they like?"

Herschel considered, studying the twinkling pinpoints of crystal cold light. "There's millions of them . . . like—"

"Bits of glass," Solly said, drawing up his knees.

"Or specks of sand?" Berta asked in a hushed, wistful voice, looking up. "Like in the Torah. Countless . . . as God promised Abraham."

It got quiet again; Solly spoke so softly, impossibly so, it might have been a dream. Those stars might not exist, he was saying, but the light of their fires could still be falling, arriving, so it was not light itself but its memory.

It was like the past was coming down . . . like their past wishes, and dreams, not the reality of another cold starry night in Germany.

The past was coming.

Solly reached out to grasp their hands; all looked up, their throats white and vulnerable in the moonlight, their words puffs of vapor.

"We'll get Mama out!"

"We'll get out of Germany!"

"The first one out will bring the others over."

They spun in a circle; Berta's thick dark hair furled around as the stars whirled and streaked.

"We'll make it. I know we will."

It was going to be so wonderful, but then things started to fall apart right after the seder. Instead of Solly, only I got to France. I did not want to. But as soon as I arrived, I started to work to save my family.

Herschel closed his diary and stood on the bench beneath his cell's high window. He craned his neck but could see no moon.

"Forgive me," he said to the blank pages of his diary.

His attorney Szwarc bought all the newspapers he could gather that next morning. The lawyer flipped through them, spotting his name, nodding.

But by 9 A.M., he was angrily pushing through crowds in the freezing drizzle. It was not the change in the weather, as much as that in the papers, that chilled him.

He shoved at the crowd. When a man moved and a woman backed away, he grunted; the article on one of the front pages still rankled: "Two undistinguished local lawyers have been engaged, but the Paris Jewish community wants the better-known Maitre Moro Giafferi, former minister, to take over the case of the boy who shot the embassy official."

"I could have saved him," Szwarc would tell his listeners in a few years. After the war the stories would grow even more. "Who knows?" he'd say. "Maybe if he'd stayed with us, we could have changed history."

Looking for someone to blame, he turned and grabbed his partner.

"What?" Vessine-Larue gasped.

Szwarc pushed him into the Rue d'University where the Alma Clinic stood, stolid and serene, its caryatids unconcerned under stone balconies; discolored bronze stanchions calmly held the oval glass orbs that flanked the wood and brass doorways.

In front, two men emerged from a long black Mercedes. A nun with a wide white wimple stood at the top of the steps, her hands up her sleeves.

Szwarc pushed and cried out to get through. Reporters turned around.

"It's them!"

"Grynszpan's lawyers."

"Have you seen your client?" one called.

"Where are his parents?" another demanded.

A man in a slicker asked ecstatically, "Do you think this will bring on war between France and Germany?"

Szwarc drew to attention. Solemnly raising his right hand, he said, "Now." Vessine-Larue opened a black umbrella over Szwarc, who placed his other hand in front of his stomach. It got quiet and Szwarc spoke, knowing he would make the reporters feel as bad as he did, as frustrated as he was, with everything.

"It would be unfair to our client to reveal anything this early."

As the reporters cried out in consternation, Szwarc's

eyes glittered. He exhaled. "I'm going to Fresnes to see the boy," he whispered to Vessine-Larue. "Find out who they are," he said, referring to the two men from the limousine.

Vessine-Larue trudged obediently up the wet steps.

But an officer barred him.

"I'm the assassin's attorney."

"No matter."

"But they . . ." He pointed to the two men going through the swinging door.

"They're allowed," the guard with pale gold eyes and fair hair told him.

"Why?"

He seemed impressed despite himself. "It's the Führer's personal physician and another doctor—just in by fast train from Germany."

Dr. Karl Brandt smiled bitterly as he walked in, and Dr. George Magnus of the Surgical Institute, elegant as a knife, Prussian with precision, came up the steps after him. Joseph Goebbels, the Führer's propaganda minister, had personally picked them last night and sent them forth from Germany.

The nun led them down the shinning hospital hallway. She tapped on a door, and Dr. Baumgartner, the clinic's director, called out and rose from his massive oak desk in greeting. He was as tall and elegant a man as Magnus, his hair silvery. He pursed his lips.

Brandt, small and bent over, stopped, hands

clasped behind his back, as Magnus looked over his head. "We have brought medicines," he said, lifting a leather bag.

"We have adequate supplies here," Baumgartner answered, not unkindly.

"We want to see his charts."

"We want to see him," Brandt corrected, showing his displeasure and rank simultaneously.

"Certainly." Baumgartner raised his brows but came from behind his desk, nodding and showing the way with his well-manicured hand. "Follow me."

The room they approached was dark; a nurse sat nearby. Outside was the volunteer they had used for transfusions; he lay on a gurney with a bandage on his arm, folded over his stomach, looking pleased.

Inside, in his bed the patient was asleep. Black stitches stuck out from his flesh like thorns. His hair, matted with perspiration, was light but had dried darker.

Brandt reached him first. "Turn him," he ordered Magnus. "Quickly."

The patient groaned.

"What are you doing?" Baumgartner protested.

Magnus ignored him, hunching over and crouching down as if listening.

"What did he say?"

"'Herschel'?" Magnus asked.

"Impossible!" Brandt shot back. "You're imagining things."

It took Szwarc an hour and a half to get to Fresnes from the Alma Clinic by taxi. He had documents to sign and paperwork and policies to review. Finally, he reached the cell. Outside, he walked in a circle and chewed the ends of his moustache; then he entered quickly, without knocking.

"What is it? What's happened?" Herschel cried in panic. "Who are you?"

"Your attorney. Yesterday. We met."

Herschel ran forward, hands to his mouth. "What's happening to . . ."

Szwarc said nothing. Let the client speak.

"The man, in the embassy . . ."

Szwarc allowed his face no changes.

". . . who was shot."

Very interesting, he thought, reaching for conclusions. "My assistant is checking on him."

Herschel gulped, relieved. "What about my family back in Germany? They've been expelled, I don't know where exactly!"

"We're inquiring."

Herschel plunged on. "Do you think they know? Do you think my brother, Solly, knows what I've . . . what's happened to me?"

The whole world knows, Szwarc gloated, rocking, almost swaggering. But he managed to hold it in and say sternly, "War may be declared soon." Herschel furrowed his brows and sat down suddenly. Szwarc whispered in his ear, "We have to get the whole story. To defend you."

Herschel looked away.

"Tell me. How did you get in?"

The boy looked up shyly, as if invited into the dark man's dancing eyes.

"I thought it would be hard," he said as if in wonder. "But it wasn't. It was easy."

He had not slept for days by then. He had been sick but felt better; buying the gun had given him direction. Then he had taken the Metro and, asking one or two questions, found the vast, multistoried building with its steep green copper roof. There were endless windows and dormers all along it and trees with green and yellow leaves falling in the warm morning. (He'd remember the falling yellow and green leaves forever; whenever he'd think of it, he'd feel the warmth of that morning.) There was no line yet.

He stuffed the pistol down deeper in his trousers. Others soon arrived and stood behind him. He felt like he was in a waking dream—and that he was in the grip of a force that controlled him.

At 9 A.M. a man came out and stood at a narrow side gate.

That was when Herschel panicked and decided to turn back, but bells were ringing and the gate opened.

"I have secrets," he gasped, as if to himself.

"Who do you want to see?" someone asked. "The ambassador?"

He must have said yes, for that was whom they called. But he was out. The guard said he could see the third secretary. That sounded familiar, so he agreed. But something was wrong—he did not know what. He had been sick, had not slept the night before, and knew he was not thinking clearly. An old man came, led him in, and pointed to an arched door.

"I didn't want to hurt anyone! But the man . . . he called me names! He struck me; I was going to get him to free my family or kill myself. I'd make a statement that way—and the ambassador would know, he'd tell the whole world—"

"It wasn't the ambassador you shot."

"I didn't know that! I swear I never saw him till that morning."

"But you said it was the third secretary."

"How was I to know?"

Szwarc tried a hunch. "You're lying."

He saw panic and fear as the boy squirmed and showed that trapped animal look. The lawyer pressed his advantage, leaning on the boy physically. "Why did you go there? Tell me."

Herschel pulled away. "To make a statement," he cried. "To save my family! Germany expelled them, all Polish Jews without papers. But the man in the office, I didn't know him." His voice was high and hoarse. "He shouted 'Jew'! He—"

36

"Yes? Yes?" Szwarc looked eagerly at the boy.

His voice changed, grew flat. "I've written it down. This is exactly what happened," Herschel replied, extending the diary. Szwarc looked at it doubtfully, like a dog sniffing poisoned meat. He sat down and Herschel turned away, back to the wall.

Licking his fingertip, Szwarc turned the pages, sometimes looking up at the boy, sometimes frowning as if debating with himself. Something was wrong, off-kilter. The boy, he knew, was watching him surreptitiously.

Turning the last page, Szwarc slowly closed the book and said nothing.

He got up and paced. "Only your brother, you say, what's his name?" he turned a page, "had a visa. Only Solly."

"Yes."

"So how did *you* get here?"

"I didn't want to; he—made me."

"Who made you?"

"Solly."

"I don't understand."

"We couldn't get work permits; Jews couldn't enter schools or public swimming pools. And one morning, in the market, there was a crowd, a speaker shouting about Yids. It was Passover. 'They kill our babies to paint their doorposts,' he screamed. 'Let's go,' I told Solly."

Like a crazed sentry or a wind-up toy, the young pink-faced blond boy marched back and forth, spitting out

"Jew!" He contorted his face, calling, "Unnatural beasts." He was the one who had dropped his pants, and Herschel turned away.

The boy saw Solly and stopped. Solly smiled. "Unnatural," he laughed. Solly was turning to go and said to Herschel, "I suppose he knows of what he speaks."

Solly started to laugh and did not hear the scream.

Herschel turned to his attorney. "They came for us, shouting, 'Christ killer!' and 'Jew!'

"I was grabbed, and someone grabbed Solly, but he pushed me away—hard! I stumbled under a table; people kicked. I rolled to the side. I got away, but he . . .

"'Run,' Solly screamed."

Herschel looked back; they were ripping off Solly's clothes—and they were pulling at their own belts. Herschel stumbled and fell under foot; he clawed through their legs; he could no longer see.

He panicked; he found a clear spot and jumped up; he was running.

At home Mama clawed the air; she wept. "No, not Solly. Anyone but Solly. Why not you?" she pushed Herschel aside and grabbed Sendel by the collar. "Go get him! Save him."

"But Rifkah."

"Idiot! fool!" she yelled. "Get him back for me."

Berta went to comfort her, but Mama threw her off

with a violent shake. "I hate you all," she screamed. "Solly!" she threw herself on the bed. "He's the only one I love. Solly!"

Papa glared at Herschel. "See what you've done! It should have been you."

Three days later Solly came back, dirty, bruised, and limping. At the corner he stopped and smiled, looking up at the building. He was wan and weary and wise, as if he had been away for centuries. Mama shrieked when she saw him coming up the street; she met him at the door. He wavered at the threshold and stumbled in. Mama kneeled and hugged him, opening her mouth and shutting it silently.

There were bruises on his cheek, a gash down his forehead. His left eye was swollen shut—so that the undamaged right eye, serene and blue, looked wrong. Rifkah tried to pat his cheek, but he flinched in pain; he had his right arm in a sling and three fingers dangled uselessly.

Unable to touch him, Rifkah held her hands over him, moving them back and forth as she would with the sabbath candle blessings. Then he let her hold his left hand.

"Darling," she said, leading him into the apartment. "Where were you?"

"In prison," he explained.

Herschel burned. Solly had taken his suffering.

Mama wailed. "You fought back; you fought them."

She took Solly's hand, and he winced, and she kissed his bruises. "You have to go now—before they come back for you!" Herschel and Berta started to cry. "Across any border; leave me. Go. Leave. Save yourself," Mama keened.

Someone in uniform came looking for Solly the next morning.

"Don't be scared," Solly whispered to Herschel from under the bed, as an officer filled out official forms in the hallway. Mama swore that she had thrown him out, the good-for-nothing who thought only of himself. She said she hadn't seen him for weeks.

Hands on her hips, she railed about Solly.

When the man left, Solly crawled out.

And Mama repeated that he had to go; she started throwing his clothes together, reaching for money she had hidden. She thrust a wad at him and then tore her dress.

Solly kissed the top of her head and then motioned to Herschel. They went to a corner of the room.

"I'm sorry," Herschel wept. "It should have been me—"

"No," Solly said, "I've told nobody . . . about . . ."

Lips pursed, dark profile worried, hair falling over his brow, Solly moved back and forth from the dresser to the chair on which his open valise sat. He was shoving things in. "I need you to do something for me."

Herschel nodded. "I'll never go to the boys again. I promise. I'll think only of family."

"Good," Solly smiled, but it looked like smiling hurt; he brushed Herschel's cheek.

Herschel turned to Szwarc. "We went to the station. We had to get him out of the country."

They strode under the arching metal trestles, past a furred woman who held a barking black dog. There was the screech of wheels, the excitement of trains, departure, people talking, buying magazines.

"Listen." Solly squatted and buttoned Herschel's jacket. "I can't stand the idea of you suffering."

Herschel jerked away, but Solly insisted.

"It's only going to get worse. I heard, in the next cell, a dancer . . . it was terrible what they . . . did. We're just Jews," Solly explained, "but you . . . you're that too."

Herschel hung his head and listened. It didn't make sense—Solly was telling Herschel what he had to do—slip into Belgium where they had cousins, and then go for Quiévrain, where workmen passed into France every morning—they went back and forth on a trolley, with no one looking. In Quiévrain he could get to France with no papers. He had to hide his bag, look like a workman or his son.

"But you're the one with the visa! You're the one going!"

"No, it's been revoked; it's no good. They'll come for you next—the boy in the market will send them." He passed his ticket over and drew out a brown envelope tied in string. "It's directions to Uncle Abraham's. Get to Paris, Herschel, and convince them to get us out; work, send us money—"

The whistle screeched.

"Quick!"

In the past Solly could have lifted Herschel with one swing onto the train's metal step. But Solly's side was weak; Herschel barely made it.

He reached back toward Solly. "My clothes!"

"In the valise!" Solly threw it to him.

"Berta!"

"She'll understand!"

"Mama!"

Solly just smiled.

"No!" A sob tore out of Herschel, like his heart from his breast. He fell to his knees as the dingy glass roof of the train station gave way to sky overhead. "Solly," he screamed. Pigeons exploded upward.

The figures on the platform receded and he cried, "Solly."

So it was going to be up to me to save my family. I'd do anything to get them out, suffer, steal, anything.

When Herschel stood on the platform in Paris, he looked around, but he could not tell whether anyone was expecting him. (Could the cousins back in Belgium, so glad to have gotten rid of him, not have wired he was coming?) He saw a dark man with bad skin who smiled at everyone and another fellow who shifted back and forth on his feet and cleared his throat impatiently. He looked at his watch and refused to look at Herschel.

It had to be him, Herschel decided. He was tall and unpleasant-looking, sourly sniffing the air. Herschel tried to speak, but the man looked away every time he turned his gaze to him. The boy sighed and tried again.

"Uncle Abraham?"

The man jumped as if terrified. "What kind of trick is this?"

Herschel tried to keep his thin shoulders from shivering. "Uncle Abraham!"

43

"You're not Solly!" The man pulled a photograph from his pocket. He slapped it. "He's bigger, older."

"He couldn't come; there was a problem."

"I'll show you a problem."

"Solly was caught; he . . ." Herschel wanted to cry. He had been on his own for three weeks now, and he was tired and scared, but his uncle's disgusted look stopped him.

Uncle Abraham resembled his father—in eyes and coloring—but he was taller and even a bit distinguished, what with his thin hooked nose and silver-tipped hair. "Let me see your papers."

Herschel winced. "I don't have any."

"WHAT?" Abraham roared, quickly smiling at the new folks who had come up on the platform—another train was due in. The oily dark man who looked eastern, Mediterranean, had been looking at the great overhead clock, but now stepped forward; Abraham nodded curtly. "God," he whispered through clenched teeth, "you'll get me in trouble. How did you get in?"

"At Quiévrain . . . on the border, I went over with some workmen who go over every morning and . . . Ow!"

Abraham pulled Herschel by his ear, preventing the dark man from intervening. But there was something about the man—his smile signaled that he wanted to be Herschel's friend, so the boy turned to him. "It's going to cost a lot of money to fix this," his uncle whispered hotly, looking at Herschel's passport. "A lot. We obey laws in France," he said loudly for those standing around to hear, then dropped his voice. "Did you bring any?"

Herschel shook his head.

"You'll pay me back then, hear? You'll work long and hard—"

"I want to work!" Herschel smiled rapturously. "I want to make lots of money."

The dark man skirting the edge of their conversation smiled like that was just exactly what he wanted to hear. Uncle raised his hand. Herschel jerked away. "Uncle Abraham! Please! I've been through so much."

Abraham stalked away, then turned back. He tossed Herschel his passport. "Hurry up! Get your bag!"

Herschel glanced at the dark man; his eyes continued to bathe Herschel with a warm and friendly appeal. Gratefully, he snatched up his valise and ran behind his uncle. Herschel looked back. He was glad, somehow; the dark man was following him; it was a good omen.

But what if he was Gestapo? He could have taken the train in from Germany.

They crossed ugly neighborhoods, cheerless and gray, thronged with people and four- and five-storied soot-covered buildings. As they crossed broad avenues with honking cars, buses, and carriages carrying a tide of humanity, he craned his neck up and down the tree-lined ways. No signs forbidding Jews here.

Finally, they stopped in front of a tall, ugly yellow brick building, with green metal windows and trimmings. It had eaves that stuck out over the street, with odd wooden brackets. Herschel collapsed on the shallow cement front steps. But Abraham jerked him toward the door, which was missing some of its glass panes.

"In here."

He looked about. The dark man had disappeared.

There was a narrow lobby but no doorman; a few steps led to a door that was propped open. Herschel followed his uncle up the central staircase. His bag hit the balusters step after step. Finally, they reached the third floor and embarked down a maze of dark halls with damp unpainted cement walls, muffled voices, and smells of cooking. Gratefully, Herschel noted that most of what he heard was German. French was not easy. They reached a door with an oval of opaque glass; it said, "Maison Albert," the words spread across it like medals on a hero's chest. "My French name," Abraham coughed into his hand, as if embarrassed by the ornate painted fussiness. He turned the glass knob.

Herschel entered a narrow hall papered in lilac; a red rug lay on the wood floor. The place was clean, though it looked like no one had painted the reddish woodwork in years. He could hear excited babbling from an open door at the end of the hall, and a pleasant-looking woman in low heels emerged with a shriek. She waddled up, clasping and unclasping her dimpled hands. She smoothed her brown dress, which pinched her like a sausage skin.

46

"Solly?"

Herschel shook his head, and his aunt, who had a kindly powdered face with stark penciled eyebrows, looked up at her husband. He rolled his eyes and rubbed his forehead. "The momzer, my bastard brother, sent another. The boy's illegal."

Chawa bent down and lifted Herschel's chin. Powder flaked like flour off her moist skin. "Don't cry," she whispered, squeezing his cheeks. "That's all right. You're welcome here."

He nodded, smiling, but choked, unable to speak. Kindness always undid him.

"What's your name?"

"Herschel Feibel."

"I'm glad you are here, Herschel. Come," she stretched her hand out, squeezed his, and raised her penciled eyebrows. She led him to a paneled wooden door that was half open.

"You'll be in here." The room was yellow, narrow as a hall, with bolts of fabric standing on end along the right-hand wall, a dressmaker's dummy and a cot at the end. Above the cot was a window with no blinds that looked out on a building across the street. Sunlight filtered through the window's grime, and a single light bulb dangled from the ceiling. "It's your uncle's work room," she said. "I hope you won't mind."

Herschel put down his valise. "It's wonderful," he said in awe, and Chawa beamed. She took his hand again and held it up to her lips and kissed it.

"This way. He's here!" she announced, rapping on the door frame as she pulled him into a brightly lit square room. Heat hissed from a corner stove. The walls had mauve and black patterned paper, and a rounded bay window stuck out over the street. A calendar advertising soap was tacked on the wall, and the mismatched furniture was dark and heavy, some missing pieces of veneer. Cloth doilies that looked like soiled snowflakes were everywhere.

Two or three adults, languid in red-and-gold upholstered chairs, turned around slowly.

"Meet your uncle Solomon," Chawa said, motioning to the big man in a chair. Solomon had dark eyes, a large nose, and swarthy shadowed cheeks; he was balding, with strands of hair shiny with grease. He did not speak but kept his eyes on Herschel as he listened to his brother Abraham.

"He's not the one with the visa. But the idiots sent him."

Solomon pursed his fish lips, then he stroked his chin as if summoning his namesake's wisdom.

"And your aunt Rita."

She had the smashed-in face of a Pekinese, with hair too black to be real. She looked him over and sniffed.

"Don't worry," said Solomon, turning back to Abraham. "They'll never notice he's not the one with the visa."

"You don't think?"

He made a dismissive gesture. "If you're not a

Frenchman . . . bah!"—he mimed batting at an insect—
"we're all the same to them."

"Maybe," Abraham mused. He dropped into a low
upholstered chair and grabbed a thick white plate with
bread and herring and started to push it into his
mouth, till he choked. "Chawa. Something to drink!"

She darted out of the room and returned with a
thick glass with a clear liquid in it. Abraham took it immediately and raised it, eyeing Herschel.

"You'll do what I say?"

"Yes, sir."

Chawa clasped her hands together. "Such nice
manners."

Abraham grunted, putting down his drink. All at
once the adults picked up their plates again and started
to speak.

Content in the heat and babble of voices, Herschel
took in his surroundings.

There was a caned wooden chair along the wall and
he perched on it, looking at the table with the cake and
cups and plates. "Go on," Chawa laughed. "Help yourself." There was bread and sauerkraut and cheese. He
started toward it, then stopped.

Chawa looked up from her full plate. "Can I get
you something else?"

He shook his head, feeling virtuous, but he had a
hard time eating anything that was fancy. She put her
food down, embarrassed. "Poor thing," she cooed. His
uncle glared. "No special treatment here."

Herschel agreed.

They slowly ate their fill; the men belched, and the women laughed.

Aunt Rita put down her plate and sighed deeply. The men crossed their hands over their stomachs. Rita reached for the cake.

"They spit on Jews in the street," Herschel said softly.

Everyone looked up. He continued, "Rats are everywhere and Germans treat us . . ."

They looked disgusted, as if he had just passed gas.

"They pick on us for nothing. They beat Solly up and he came home, his clothes full of shit and piss!"

"Please," said Rita, her flat, pushed-in lapdog's face unhappy as she spit seed cake into her napkin. "I'm eating."

Even Aunt Chawa looked unhappy.

"Is that what your brother's family's like?" Aunt Rita asked of Abraham and Solomon. "It looks like he's the same way," she said, pointing at Herschel's pants and holding her nose.

They started laughing.

Herschel ran from the room, and Chawa went after him.

My aunts and uncles were so upset, seeing how much I suffered in Germany. But I did not have the right papers; they said it was going to be hard for me to bring over my family.

The boy was lying. Of that Szwarc was sure. But why? And how could a yokel like him have brought on such a crisis between France and Germany? When the lawyer looked into the boy's eyes now, he saw disturbing broken things, wrecks of souls, bad dreams, darkness spilling. He did not like being in the cell with him.

He had to leave. But just then he heard a knock and the turn of a key. The door opened and Vessine-Larue was let in. His too-blue suit had dark streaks where the rain had wet it; his flesh was pale, his hair frazzled and orange, like a child's drawing of electricity. Herschel rushed to him.

"Stop!" Szwarc called to his partner. He put his finger to his lip and tilted his head.

They went to a corner, and Szwarc spoke behind his hand. "I think the boy and the man he shot knew each other."

"How could they?"

"It's just a feeling. Look at him!"

Herschel hovered, anxiously.

"When I came in, he asked about vom Rath. If he loved his family, he would have asked about them first. And the way he kept telling me, again and again, that he didn't know him . . ."

"But he's . . . and the German—"

"Exactly." Szwarc raised his eyebrows.

They both turned to Herschel.

"We need to ask you some questions." Vessine-Larue sat and pulled out a pad, ready to take notes.

"Tell me about your life in Paris," Szwarc began mildly. "After you entered, did you straighten out your papers, get a visa?"

Herschel's voice broke. "Uncle tried to."

"And?"

"He took me to the Jewish Committee, and they said they'd help."

"Did they?"

"No." His face clouded. "Though they said they would."

"And?"

It wasn't until spring, several months later, that the family, or Abraham, got a letter. Herschel came home to find his uncle pacing back and forth in the Maison Albert's hallway, throwing his arms up in a rant. Aunt Chawa had to tell him what the matter was. The Jewish Committee had failed to pass on the paperwork. It was an oversight, they said.

"It'll be all right," she soothed. "Come help me make dinner."

Abraham left and returned a few hours later, saying he had taken care of things. He wouldn't explain further, and no one spoke during the meal.

A few weeks later, in early summer, a letter addressed to Herschel arrived. It contained a receipt from the Interior Ministry. It acknowledged that he had applied for a residency permit to stay in France. He needed a visa too, to show he had entered legally. Final notification of his status would come by mail from the Ministry.

"That was all your uncle did?" Szwarc asked, disdain in his voice.

"Yes." Herschel looked at the floor.

"So you were still not official, but at least you had proof that you had applied for a change of status. You should have gone back to Germany to await word."

"I couldn't," Herschel said.

"Why?"

"When I left, I did not go through emigration — I did not get my passport stamped, so it was illegal for me to be out of Germany. Uncle found out that maybe I could apply for a waiver at the consulate, which did small things too unimportant for the embassy. So he made me go there once a week. If I went alone, he said, they would pity me. But the lady did not like Jews. 'No openings,' she'd say at the end of the day. She hated me."

"So," Szwarc began in a tone that one might use to chat about the weather. "Was it there, in the consulate, that you met him?"

"Who?"

"Vom Rath — the man you shot!"

"No," the boy shouted angrily. "You've got it wrong. We never met before yesterday. I told you."

"Sorry." Szwarc backed up and exchanged looks

with Vessine-Larue. "Tell us what you did while you waited for your papers. Did you play, make friends?"

"No! I worked. I tried to earn money. I worked. For my family."

"Doing what?"

Herschel didn't answer.

"Look at him," Szwarc whispered to Vessine-Larue. "See how he turns away; how he can't stop moving. Watch his hands twist. He's lying."

"I worked," Herschel cried. "I made money."

"How?"

It was through Dothan—that was the dark man who had followed them from the train station; he was waiting at the bottom of the steps early one morning when Herschel came down. Dothan smiled and came up to Herschel, extending his hand like they were already best friends. His black hair curled over his dark forehead and ears, and a cigarette dangled from his full lips. His skin was pitted, but except for that he was nice looking.

"Live up there?" Dothan asked, standing so close that Herschel had to step back. He laughed nervously. Dothan's eyes were brown and sincere. He could not be a Nazi. "So how do you like this country?"

"Very nice. I like it here."

"There is much to see, isn't there?"

Herschel nodded. But he had hardly ventured out, scared of his French and everything else. He just spent his time sweeping up his uncle's room and waiting around till he was needed to fetch something. Brooding and biting his nails to the quick. Worrying that he was not doing anything for his family. Not knowing how to begin. He had sorted buttons that morning. Uncle Abraham said he was too foolish to go out on his own.

"You must have lots of friends . . ."

Herschel shook his head.

"No?" Dothan seemed amazed and looked him up and down. "A nice-looking chap like you?"

Herschel blushed. The word chap fascinated him.

"I bet you'd like to earn a little extra spending money."

"I would! I need to! I have family to support! But . . ." His voice fell. "I can't. I don't have papers for a work permit."

"Poor luck," Dothan said. "Bet you're bored, need something to do?"

Herschel looked at the ground. "I work for my uncle occasionally."

"The man who met you at the train station?"

Herschel nodded.

"He seemed nice."

Herschel said nothing.

Dothan started to whistle and said, "Well, I guess I should be going."

Herschel watched him leave and was happy when Dothan suddenly turned back toward him. "Son, I have an idea."

"What?" Herschel walked over.

"Maybe you can work for me—and I can just slip you the money, without telling anybody. You wouldn't turn me in, would you?"

Herschel was touched by his trust. "No! Never!"

Dothan smiled. "Papers are for fools, not bright boys like you." He waved Herschel over to the stoop. Herschel sat and felt excited and warm as Dothan placed his hand on Herschel's wrist and scraped it with his fingernail. His senses sang. "Maybe we could go some place and talk?"

"Sure!"

He followed Dothan happily; they stopped to get an ice—and then Dothan even bought him something to drink. "Mind, don't tell your aunt I'm corrupting you," Dothan said, lifting his glass toward Herschel. "Cheers." They drank and Dothan winked. The wine made Herschel feel warm.

"What would you like me to do?" Herschel asked, finishing his glass. Dothan had gone silent. He was just sitting at the café table, rolling a cigarette, chewing his lip, and watching the passersby. He seemed most interested in young boys. Herschel tried to get his attention again, repeating his question.

Dothan turned and his face lit up. "Thought you'd never ask!" They got up and Herschel felt dizzy. "Watch it, my friend!" Dothan put his arm around his neck and asked, "Not used to drinking much? Sweet."

It felt good. He felt giddy, that such a handsome man could like him. He liked the way that Dothan held onto him and steered him down the street. Dothan took him to a room that didn't look like much of an office. Just a bed and washstand.

"Do you live here?"

"No," Dothan said, undoing his shirt. "I just use it occasionally."

He removed his tie. "Come here."

Herschel came over and sat next to him. Dothan pulled him closer. "I like you."

It was too good to believe.

"You're so handsome, Herschel," the man said, eyeing him up and down, running his hand down Herschel's arm. "Such nice smooth skin." He undid one of Herschel's shirt buttons and put his hand in. "Any hair yet? No! Good." He sat up again and kissed him. Herschel nearly swooned. Dothan looked pleased. "Many an older gentleman would pay handsomely for visits from someone as young as you."

"Oh?" He pretended not to understand. "What would I do?"

"Not much. Just what they wanted you to—take off your clothes, let them touch you."

Herschel exhaled. It was relaxing, giving in. This time he gasped when Dothan touched him.

"Now, now," Dothan soothed. "Don't be alarmed. It doesn't mean anything . . . it's just a way . . . to make money." His bright liquid eyes reassured. "It doesn't mean anything."

Herschel nodded.

The man moved closer, and his finger stroked

Herschel's throat. He undid another button and put one cool hand down Herschel's shirt. Dothan's voice was hypnotic as he circled Herschel's nipple; his other hand became a snake. Herschel shuddered as it traveled across his cheek.

"Nice," Dothan teased. "Not even the beginnings of a beard." He had Herschel on his back and was treating him like a child; like a patient mother, Dothan began to undress him.

Herschel smiled as Dothan got up.

He was dark and had hair rising up in a column in the middle of his chest. He was handsome. He came back over to the bed and starting stroking Herschel's bottom.

"I bet it's like a baby's."

"I never . . ." Herschel said, starting to pull away.

"It'll be fun. Here." He lifted the boy's legs and moved forward.

"Please, no—"

"Now, Herschel! Just relax. I'll show you something."

Herschel fell back against the wall and started to pitch, to struggle, but the man was on top of him; his face was in Herschel's. "Shut up," Dothan cried, his eyes closed to slits. His face was pitted and his breath smelled of garlic. He slapped Herschel, who cried out as Dothan grimaced, yelling obscene things, slapping at Herschel's flanks, showing his teeth. It seemed to last an eternity—and Herschel hardly knew he was crying.

When it was done, Dothan collapsed.

He got up to smoke.

Herschel turned his burning eyes on Dothan.

"Now don't pout. I just wanted a preview." Dothan rolled his lower lip, assuming an air of hurt gravity. "To see what our clients would be getting."

"I thought you liked me!"

"I do!"

Herschel shook his head and leaped off the bed. It was all a lie. No one loved anybody. Dothan lay back down; Herschel looked about wildly for his underwear. He looked under the bed, in the pile of Dothan's clothes in a chair.

"Here," Dothan said, producing the shorts like magic.

Herschel swiped at the underwear and cried, "I hate you."

"No, you don't—you like me. A lot!" Lying in bed, supporting himself on his elbows, the man drowsily watched the boy button and tuck and run his fingers through his hair. He turned to leave.

"Oh, come back," Dothan encouraged him. "No harm done." He held up some francs. "Come here."

Herschel shook his head and stood by the door.

"OK, go. You're a fool. You've got talent—a nice face too," he mused, crushing the cigarette out and sighing. "Thanks for the fun. And remember, if you ever want to make some money, just come over. I'll be here."

Outside, Herschel did not know where to go, what to do, what to think. If Dothan came out and apologized, he'd forgive him.

But it grew dark. And Herschel grew tired waiting.

"Don't you feel well?" Aunt Chawa asked him, touching her hand to his forehead when he got home. "No fever," she said.

Which showed how much she knew. He just stood inside the door, knocking his head at the doorpost, as the burning shame consumed him. He was angry with himself, with Dothan, with his aunt for not understanding. And with his uncle, who looked in on him later as he lay on his bed with his clothes on, face to the wall. Abraham shook his head and said, "Never seen anyone so lazy."

Even if Dothan came over and begged, never again would he do such things.

But that night, after he undressed and closed the door, strange lewd scenes burned in his brain and licked at him. A sickness rose in Herschel, a hunger. It propelled him out of bed the next morning and to the mirror in the bathroom when Aunt Chawa and Uncle Abraham were out. He watched his own face, which flushed and then paled. Who was this chap staring back? It was no use. He went out to the street. Winter was ending, and green was beginning to show in the trees. Dothan strode toward him.

"Ready?" he asked, smiling.

"Ready."

"I hated my work," Herschel cried to his attorneys in a ragged voice. "I only did it to support my family."

But no. For even though the men to whom Dothan sent him were mostly old and fat and had drooping breasts like old ladies, still Herschel savored the sense of walking down the street at night—I'm going to see friends, he'd tell Aunt Chawa and Uncle Abraham. He walked along excitedly, as if he had a secret, a key to taboo things. He felt dangerous with youth, willingness, guilt, and duty.

He shivered as he ran down the street.

"How disgusting," he would tell himself when the old men opened the door. "I hate it." But he grew excited as the door closed and he took his clothes off, feeling he was no longer Herschel Grynszpan, not the sad powerless boy he'd been back in Germany. With the night he grew powerful and rich as they begged and pleaded, loving his starved eyes, his underdeveloped body. He'd make them suffer for their need, what they made him do, breaking his word to Solly.

But then, for a moment, kindness would come to him. It is possible, he would think. For a moment he would believe. But then the men faltered; they apologized and gave him money.

I made lots of cash and sent it home to my parents; it was for them that I worked, not me.

Dothan was pleased and, with the skills of a match-maker, sent a smiling Herschel Grynszpan to a German officer one evening.

"He'll be good to you, if you're good to him," Dothan promised. "He's rich, I think."

The first time Herschel waited, hands together. The hotel room was dark, as he had been told it would be. As directed, he had knocked and entered. He stood patiently, without getting restless. He felt like prey. He felt the heat of the man moving in the dark, felt the German's richness exuding from his skin as he circled Herschel. Then the man went away.

A light came on.

The man was lying on a metal bed; he was huge, hairy, handsome. Herschel felt his blood rush to his face, as the man motioned him over. He felt the man's stare, then heard him sigh. The man stood up and bent Herschel over. The look on the man's cruel face left no doubt. Herschel dropped his pants.

He nearly fainted. The man shouted and slapped his flanks, "Whore! Filth! I'll show you."

Herschel swooned, wanting to say thank you, as he felt a world open and his soul disappear. The pain was important. In his mind's eye, up on the ceiling, he could imagine how it looked, and the thought excited him; it must be what God felt, as He looked down on His Earth and saw justice occurring.

Punish me! Herschel begged, lifting up his head, his eyes rolled back, his mouth a beast's.

The German swore. It was the filthy Jew's fault for wanting it—so he slapped the boy's flesh, shouted, hit him with his hand. He'd show him. It was wrong. But right too. They were having their reward and punishment simultaneously.

It became a routine, like darkness falling. Herschel was called back again and again to his German, to this one customer, this one only. They both knew what was happening in the shabby hotel room where they came to seek both solace and destruction. The man had to impress his flesh on Herschel, hot wax and a seal.

"I'll show you, I'll stop you," the German hissed.

"Yes, yes," Herschel cried through clenched teeth.

"Look at him," Szwarc said, nudging his partner. "He's nervous as a cat; I wonder what he's thinking?"

But one day there was no order, no word from the German. There was no fuel, no fire, no flesh. "Why?" Herschel asked Dothan, almost in tears. "Why has he stopped? Has he left town? Doesn't he like me?"

"Sure he does!" Dothan consoled. "Poor thing," he said, chucking Herschel under his chin. "Not to worry." He paused thoughtfully, trying to explain. "It's like needing a rest, a vacation. Like a man going back to his wife, his duty."

"I don't understand."

But Dothan shook his head, promised with his eyes, and answered as if he knew that he was speaking wisely. "He'll be back, mon cher. And once he's left his wife, his work, or whatever it is that he feels he has to do, he'll need you more than ever. He will. Believe me."

Herschel opened his mouth; he felt a vacuum, a void; he needed . . . he did not know what to do. The others—the old soldiers, the married men—wouldn't do anymore. He needed to leave. Maybe go back to . . .

"So did you make any friends?"

"I beg your pardon?"

"Friends."

Herschel twisted.

"Did you make any?"

He blinked at Szwarc, at Vessine-Larue. "What do you mean?"

"Who did you know? Who did you associate with—we need a list of names of people to interview about you."

"Oh." Herschel paused. "I knew no one." His eyes cleared. "Just Nathan, really."

"Who's he?"

Nathan Kaufman had red hair, green eyes, blotchy freckled skin, a big nose, and protruding teeth. He knew everybody in the apartment block and talked as if Herschel did too. Nathan lived with his family on the same floor as Aunt Chawa and Uncle Abraham. He invited Herschel to come along with him to his job washing dishes in a cellar restaurant on the next street.

As they walked, Nathan offered him a cigarette but did not laugh when Herschel choked. "Gosh," Nathan said, "you're an innocent."

Herschel wanted to speak, to tell Nathan everything. If he knew what he had done and all he had been through, Nathan would be in awe, envious, maybe. But Nathan did not listen.

"I'm going to be a jazz musician," he shouted to a pretty blond girl they passed in the street. She shook her hair and laughed. Nathan told Herschel how his stepfather would not let him. "It's horrible," he said. "He laughs at me!" But he'd be famous one day! Nathan stopped and his fingers mimed playing an invisible saxophone as he danced in the street. Just wait and see!

Herschel saw himself in the future, outside a club — with posters of Nathan on the wall. "We were friends," he'd tell the crowd. "He knows me."

Nathan was still miming on imaginary keys, twisting and swaying. The girl said, "Crazy."

Nathan smiled at her and ran down some steps. Herschel followed and sat on a stool in the hot kitchen as Nathan talked and talked. But when the boss's wife brought in a tray stacked full of dirty dishes, she barked, "Stop clowning. And who is he?"

Herschel blushed and crept up the steps to the street. Nathan came out an hour and a half later, and they went to meet Nathan's friends down the street.

Sometimes, if Nathan had to work late, Herschel would just go first to Cafe Tout Va Bien in Rue St. Denis. By ten Nathan would show up with other Jewish boys from his soccer league. They joked and smoked, spoke of school and films and jobs. Those boys had no secrets, no longings, no foreign families.

Herschel was shy, then giddy, and laughed at the dirty jokes they told; they tried to buy wine, but jus d'orange was all the waiters would sell them. The waiters popped towels at the boys and ignored them as they threw coins or acted out scenes from films. They bounced a ball off their elbows and heels, whistled at the women, and hooted and threw bread sticks at the silent, effeminate men (some of whom wore makeup) who sometimes strutted past or who ran like beaten dogs, melting away like fog in a breeze. The brazen ones who made eyes at them and wiggled their fannies made Herschel blush, but those who ran by, eyes averted, reminded him of Jews back home, trying not to be seen.

He could not taunt them. So the boys, Nathan's friends, made fun of him or told him was too good and called him "rabbi."

The silent shadow men passed by nearly every evening; some stopped and talked with the prostitutes in heavy makeup and cloche hats and tight red dresses who at night, and even some mornings, patrolled that part of the street.

Everyone in the cafes and apartment blocks along the way watched them and others stream in and out of the El Dorado Dance hall at the corner by the empty department store building. The El Dorado dominated the neighborhood, with its noise, its comings and goings, the frequent wailing presence of the police. It cost to go through its horseshoe-shaped doorway, which was lit with garish green and yellow lamps. Festooned with tinsel, the door, always swallowing and disgorging folks, resembled a sea anemone.

"Promise you'll never go there," Aunt Chawa had pleaded with Herschel, pulling her hems down, as they walked by one morning.

"Promise," he answered.

He thought of that (and felt guilty) every time he went in, using the spending money that she secretly passed to him, whispering, "Don't let your uncle see." He followed Nathan and his friends past the wooden turnstile, greasy with the touch of thousands of hands, and surrendered his green ticket to the crone at the gate. After that, they'd file through an arch with a velvet hanging. Then Nathan and his friends scattered into the huge room with a vaulted ceiling to find girls to dance with; Herschel, trying not to look nervous, smiled as he watched dancers spin in the smoky dream. Tinny music played and light swirled down from the glass balls rotating on the ceiling. He was too embarrassed to dance, standing instead in dismay, trying to fit in, as he lurked in the shadows of the sagging balcony.

He froze when a man with eyes for other men passed him. It was like a searchlight turned his way. They could see under his skin, like one Jew could tell another, even if that Jew was pretending to be a Pole or a German. Some men winked at him.

Others searched the darkness for other men. The feeling they gave him made his skin hot and his insides weak; he felt giddy noticing two men meet, whisper together, and leave.

Old men looked at boys; boys stuck out their chins. Some came and left together; Herschel knew what they were doing. The boys got power and prestige, not to mention money, from the old men.

But not everyone knew what they were up to. Not Nathan and his friends.

The secret made Herschel's heart speed.

The first time he saw the old woman at the door smile was when two men—those who did not charge (bar boys called them "pansies") came in. (Those who charged were called "Arabs" on the street.) The woman hugged them to her hollow chest and let them through the turnstile for free.

The younger man was tall, pale, and thin; his long dark hair fell greasy and lank. He held a cane in his twisted right hand; he linked his other through the arm of his friend, who was older, shorter, and had a deeply furrowed forehead, small eyes, and cleft chin. He made his steps match the tiny ones of his gaunt, limping friend.

A dark voluptuous woman with heavy black hair and a blouse cut low like a gypsy's came their way; she had a very red mouth and laughed as the thin one, lining himself up carefully with a wicker chair, held onto the arms and then let go, dropping with a cry into the seat. He gasped; the wicker creaked.

The woman bent over and kissed him. Looking about, jangling her bangles, she hiked up her skirts. Nathan and his soccer friends came up from the crowd, shrieked, whistled, and stamped their feet; she smiled and winked. They watched her, but Herschel watched the men. The older one's lashless dark eyes stayed on his friend; he was so thin and had desiccated leathery skin, his legs and arms like a skeleton's.

He tried not to look. But he could not help himself.

To scratch his nose, the skinny man lifted his arm and moved it as jerkily as a puppet's. His birdlike eyes darted to catch everything. He said something, and the woman roared, shaking her breasts; the older man smiled. And the skinny man smiled back at him, their eyes igniting. They created a space like vaporous air around a fire that wavered and danced; it was just for them.

After a bit, after a swallow of his drink, the thin man gasped. He lurched and coughed; his face paled, making his mouth seem red, as if with blood or lip-stick. And there was blood in the handkerchief that he held to his lips. He bent over, as if the cough would break him.

With a gasp he finally stopped coughing. When he did, the other man lifted his friend's hand to his lips like a chalice and kissed it.

Nathan's friends stopped and looked, but Herschel's skin was on fire.

"Vomit," one of Nathan's friends cried out. "Look at them. They're sick! Disgusting!"

"Shhh," Herschel said, spinning around.

Love. That was what was between them; the thought warmed like brandy.

"They're perverted—diseased!"

"But that's what they say about Jews!" Herschel blurted out.

Nathan's friend averted his eyes. "It's not the same thing." He lurched up and deliberately bumped the other table. And the man, the older one, looked up.

"It was not me," Herschel wanted to say as he looked toward the older man. But he could not speak. Men could love each other.

The older one said something and got his friend to his feet. He wavered and weaved, as his friend fussily tucked a black-and-white muffler around his neck. Before they left, they turned back. Herschel's eyes begged: "Don't go. Stay. Please."

"Where are you going?" Nathan asked him.

Outside, Herschel looked both ways, but the men he wanted to know were nowhere to be seen. Something was in the air, something wistful and silvery and sad, something wanting to be found. Herschel thought of the German; how he had . . .

But that was not right.

The moon rose, and he remembered the stars he had seen that night outside Hanover with Berta and Solly. He kept walking, unable to get the two men out of his mind; they got mixed up with everything, the way things entered his dreams while he was sleeping. He felt the stir of revelation, the brush of foreign worlds, wings.

He hugged himself and moonlight silvered the street. Something was strange and unnerving about light at night. It gave you second sight and let you witness things not normally seen—does love do that? he wondered suddenly. Light at night. He held up his hand, looking at it as if it, or he, was suddenly capable of new things.

Aunt Chawa was up, hunched over a plate. Her hair was in a net and her face shiny with grease. He did not want to speak, just sneak to his room, to examine the new feeling, like some new purchase, a secret luxury. "Been with your girlfriend?"

Herschel gasped, angry that she could think such dirty things.

"Can't fool me," she said, chewing. "Write your Mama; it'll make her happy."

"Not Mama!"

"I know," Chawa said, raising her palm. He tried

not to wince at the grease on her face as she kissed him and went off to sleep.

He slipped down to the window at the end of his narrow, unlit room. As he stood next to the dressmaker's dummy and looked down, he could see a man walking alone in the pale light, his shadow undulating alongside him.

Herschel kissed the air. He moved around the narrow room, finally digging into a pile of papers, unfolding several sheets; in the moonlight he took them to the window to read.

A letter. Like a scent, its message hung in the air.

"Berta." Closing his eyes, he heard her voice, felt her presence, her dim imploring eyes in the shape of her handwriting. He put her letter, like a hand, against his cheek.

He sighed; it was wrong to believe in other things.

And wrong to love someone who was not family. "That man you went to see—from the embassy . . ." Herschel reached for Vessine-Larue and said, "Tell me about him."

Vessine-Larue blinked.

"How he is, how he's doing."

"Why?"

Herschel just reached for the paper in his attorney's hand.

In Berlin, the propaganda minister of the thousand-year Reich grimaced as he read the telegram that lay on his vast desk.

> *The condition of Secretary of Legation Ernst vom Rath is quite grave, due mostly to internal bleeding and damage to the spleen. The consequences of the considerable loss of blood will be treated with further blood transfusions. The French, under Dr. Baumgartner, Paris, have done well and may save the life of our man.*
> *Drs. Magnus and Brandt*

Upset, Herr Doktor Joseph Goebbels brushed the paper to the floor, like an insect or a Jew.

And picked up his pen. It could not be happening that way.

History, he wrote on thick cream-colored sheets, *was made as Ernst vom Rath, distinguished member of a distinguished family, died 9 November 1938 at the hand of a vicious Jewish assassin.*

There—that was better.

Whenever the world presented the minister with something that was askew, he started by writing the reverse. (That was his job, after all, to use words to change things.) As he wrote, and the pen scratched in the silence, Goebbels felt the rising force of fate, the necessity of the moment, and the brimming tide of history. He moved his hand over his slicked-back hair, icing on his nearly fleshless skull. What he wrote, he knew, would become true.

Vom Rath died as he lived—in service to his country. He came in early every day at the embassy and left late. He took his job for his country seriously.

It did not matter who vom Rath had been, but what he—Goebbels—made him into. He pictured, with glee, the scene as it must have unfolded in the embassy—the meeting of the Jew assassin Herschel Grynszpan and his German victim Ernst vom Rath.

"The French fail again," Ernst had called out, stepping up that day—evening, actually—into the consulate's small lobby.

Jorns, who supervised vom Rath, had offered him a ride home, as they left the embassy together. But vom Rath still had a few things to do, he had explained, fanning out the letters in his hand.

On his way home he often walked the dozen or so

blocks from the embassy to the consulate, so he could deliver mail that had been misdirected to his office.

"I don't know why you do that," Jorns said. "They're not going to notice or reward you."

"It doesn't matter," Ernst replied, stepping away from his boss's car. He knew Jorns pitied him.

Once inside the consulate Ernst stepped forward and handed the envelopes to the pretty blond secretary who always stayed late to flirt with him.

She looked up from her desk at the bottom of the spiral stairway. A boy stood in front of her, but he obviously wasn't important. Still, he looked oddly familiar to Ernst, and as memory rose, he burned with a familiar sensation. A pleasing tingle. Like curry. What luster he had! And with that dark hair, those waiflike eyes, and slim, undeveloped body, the boy looked eastern, exotic. Ernst thought of India, the heat. Sweat prickled the base of his neck. "Behave," a voice like his father's warned him.

How miscast the boy seemed. He looked up at Ernst, as if for help; then hope melted. His dark eyes widened; he tossed his hair back and opened his mouth.

I am not what you see, Ernst thought, sure his features cast him as a cold German professional.

Herschel tried not to stare at the man, who obviously was important. He pursed his lips and tried to toss his shoulders provocatively, like a glamorous actress in a film. He looked back once as he left the building.

"Who was he?" Ernst asked matter-of-factly as he walked to the window.

The secretary's face was dead white, vermilion lips vampirish, her eyes inviting him to malice. "Just a Jew trying to get in where he's not wanted."

"A Jew!"

"Yes." She winked.

Ernst looked away. Poor thing. Ernst did not know the official policy of Berlin—those things were quite hush-hush; some people—Jorns—knew and knew not to tell him. But now was no time for a Jew to be going back to Germany, Ernst knew.

He smiled at the secretary and told her how nice she looked. She looked down demurely and then back up to answer, but he was too quick; he had left the building.

Those months before Ernst vom Rath had been troubled by dreams.

And longings that he could share with nobody.

For if he gave in to them, something terrible would happen, as it had in India. So it was not until late in the afternoon or evening, when all the tasks on his to-do list were checked off, that Ernst (and the voice in his head) allowed himself to think of such things; then, like a breeze through an open window, his dreams flowed in. After work, he either went to Mademoiselle Taulin's for lessons in perfecting his French accent, stayed home to read, or went out walking in the indescribable melting colors of evening.

As he left, the porter Nagorka looked after him, knowing that, with dedication such as vom Rath's, glory awaited Germany.

With his guidebook in hand (and recollections of his other, earlier times in Paris to steer him), Ernst dutifully navigated streets, looking for the architectural details noted in the guides; he paused in churches and museums, in search of the inspiration and uplift known to be found in such settings. Then he would retrieve the silver pencil (a gift from Mademoiselle Taulin) and, like another task done, check off the sights he had seen, circling those worth a return visit, putting a question mark at those he did not understand or found puzzling. Later, at his lesson, or at tea to which he would take Mademoiselle once a week, he'd question her. If it was something too indelicate to speak of, Ernst turned to his fat black encyclopedias. It was good to have endless things to decipher about the French and their city.

It was a failing, he knew (he had many), but as spring progressed, he was finding it easier to wander. This was not good—for he had things to achieve. Yet when he looked down alleys where young boys lounged, blowing smoke rings, trailing a sense as tantalizing as fragrance behind them, he wanted to throw down his guidebook. Then, he felt he was on sand, and waves and currents were undercutting him.

He had to hold back, no matter how difficult, like not touching a place that itched. He had to resist. For if he did not, he was lost. It had a logic like physics. The more he scratched, the more he would itch.

Ernst turned twenty-nine that spring. With a desperation that was disabling, he looked at the boys and wondered, "Will things ever change for me?"

Ernst vom Rath owed certain obligations to his neighbors, to his image of himself, and to Germany. This was how he had been raised. Neither he nor his younger brothers, Gustav and Guenther, had to experiment or think. They only had to fit in, like putting on a suit of clothes laid out for them each morning.

The three vom Rath sons had seen all the photographs in the thick leather albums and had listened again and again to the stories of how dowagers with lorgnettes and gentlemen in epaulettes had regarded their father—a dashing young man sashed in gold with a trim moustache and ramrod stiff posture—as the embodiment of all that was great about Germany.

Father had done what was expected of him. He had studied and entered the civil service and for decades performed his patriotic duty. Only after he had fulfilled his obligation to the state had he turned his attention to the family's sugar factory. Ernst, as eldest, would surely follow suit; he had to set the example for his two younger brothers, who naturally looked up to him. (But they didn't, Ernst knew; when his back was turned, they joked and sniggered at his expense.) So as he grew, he knew to make choices only about little things, the color of his handkerchiefs, books for pleasure reading, and where he would spend his vacations walking. The big decisions were for his father and mother—what school to go to, what profession to choose. (Frau vom Rath would, of course, bow to her husband's greater wisdom in these things.)

As expected, Ernst had done well in school; at nineteen he had declared for the diplomatic corps at his father's prompting. ("You are not strong enough for the military," Father had said. And Ernst, not looking at his father, had wordlessly agreed. "So we'll try diplomacy.")

All knew he would succeed. For weren't they vom Raths? And wasn't his mother's brother, Roland Koester, ambassador to France? Ernst would make good, if not for himself, then for his family. And Germany. But sometimes he acknowledged that he did not fit in. Like the roll of flesh that clung to his middle and shins, doubt swaddled him. "What is wrong?" he'd sometimes wonder, as he brooded and dreamed of strange things. He prayed to wake up changed and be like everyone else, unaware of the complexities and contradictions that he alone could see. But he did not wake up changed, and sometimes he was secretly, maybe perversely, pleased to be able to see true things that others could not. Sometimes he wondered whether he was not being chosen for something else, culled from the crowd for a special destiny.

If a boy brushed by him on a late evening walk, Ernst would worry, feeling that fear of cliffs, of letting go, falling. He'd draw his shoulders up stiffly, impersonating the formal Prussian ancestors whose portraits lined the staircase back home. He'd go to his flat and lecture himself and wake up early to do deep-knee bends before going off to the embassy at dawn to work exhausted till evening. That was the way he'd achieve his goal, his whole reason for coming back to Paris.

So what was he doing out on the street?

Looking. And so was the boy. He was waiting, wasn't he?

As Ernst descended the steps of the consulate, the dark boy got up and started to walk away. As Ernst followed, a voice like his father's sounded in his head—"Behave!" it again commanded—but Ernst shook it off. The boy moved away. Ernst had to warn him not to go back to Germany.

Herschel stooped, pretending to tie his shoe. Take the first step, please. Even if it wasn't the same man who made him feel he needed to be punished. Still, the blond man had gotten under his skin; an erotic longing, a looseness, shivered in him.

In Germany nights meant sleep, but here they excited, rubbing on you like a cat, stimulating you as silk stockings might as you slipped them on and they crackled with expectancy.

Herschel stood up and looked at Ernst, then began walking.

Ernst crossed the street and followed Herschel. Herschel kept looking back, finally stopping at the front steps of the El Dorado Dance Hall, its garish holiday lights twinkling yellow and green. His throat was too dry to speak; he mouthed a greeting, but the blond man just stared. Looking back one more time, Herschel slipped inside.

Ernst vom Rath knew not to follow him. He had first come to Paris in 1934 to learn French with the sweet and lovely Mademoiselle Taulin, who would prepare him for his required foreign language exams. He had done well, so he asked the mademoiselle if he might be allowed to continue corresponding with her from Germany.

She had said yes, lowering her blue eyes, crimson tingeing her cheeks; maybe I will love her one day, he thought; but his parents, seeing her letters arrive addressed in florid purple ink, demanded that the relationship cease.

There was a scene—if one can call Ernst's request for them to reconsider a scene. When he delivered his request, he was standing, and they, like judges, were sitting at a desk.

His father withdrew and came back with his ruling the next morning. Ernst could write the Frenchwoman but only of specific things; she, in turn, could correct his French and return the letters with comments, which Ernst would then turn over to his parents. But she could expect nothing else. She was French; he German. She could do whatever she liked with the fee—give it away to the war widows, if she liked—but they would never accept her insulting charity. "She has designs on you, see?"

So the senior vom Rath paid, and Mademoiselle Taulin continued to correct his letters in red, and Ernst handed them over dutifully for his parents to read.

In French he foundered, like a drowning person. The language enthralled and unsettled him; how it made his tongue move trapped him in queasy not-black, not-white feelings. French was for fantasizing, German for governing.

"It is with great pleasure," he wrote Mademoiselle a year later, "that I tell you I am returning. I hope I can become your student again." In April 1935 he was posted to Paris to serve as secretary to his uncle Roland, the ambassador. ("A promotion, see? Work hard!") Uncle Koester treated him civilly but, to prove he was not playing favorites, did not socialize with his nephew. And Aunt Koester had plenty of other young men to serve as extras at her formal dinner parties. So evenings, he stayed in, conjugating verbs and improving his vocabulary. Occasionally, he went with Mademoiselle Taulin to the opera and regretted that his parents did not allow him to pay for her ticket. Music stirred him and moved her too. In French they laughed and discussed things they could not in German. When he clicked his heels and bowed, holding her hand like a bouquet, she looked sweet.

On the way home, urged on by the music echoing in his head, he stopped in front of bar doors, trapped and weak. The shining eyes, insinuating laughs, and elegantly limp wrists of the boys inside tempted him. They were delicate glass creatures, he dull and clumsy. When Uncle Roland died, Ernst told himself he should be glad it caused him to be called back to Germany.

Ernst waited for word of his next posting, remembering not to wring his hands, for Father considered that gesture unmanly. Ernst knew that and he knew too (how could he not?) that although he had done his job thoroughly and quietly and unostentatiously, he did not excite; when his superiors looked at Ernst, none saw the future or prophesied great things. Jorns, who had been there too, was handsome and ingratiating. Jorns was promoted. "Ernst," Jorns had said with disdain, "you try too hard. Relax and enjoy yourself." Next to Jorns, Ernst knew he was colorless as a folder and as boring.

But he had a heart, he had feelings.

At home he looked at books, lifting the tissue guard from the colored plates of exotic places he had never seen.

When still no word came, Father produced Ernst's résumé, and together one evening they looked it over closely. Father sat at the desk, Ernst at his elbow, like a waiter with a wine list. "Here," his father said, tapping the paper in the pool of golden light in the dim rich library. "This is it! Mind, this means something." His father then finished with a quick glass of schnapps, dispatched with military precision, without getting his clipped moustache wet. "You'll see."

Ernst flushed at his father's words. No doubt, it was another of Ernst's failures, but three years earlier, in 1932, he had joined the National Socialists, lured by the party's promise of order, neatness, and the fine young men marching in uniform. Oh, just to see them passing by made him believe. And in those early weeks, Ernst had found peace in their ranks; in the maleness, comfort, and camaraderie; in the mechanics of marching that dulled his mind and exalted and exhausted his body.

But having those men in the bunks right next to him kept him tossing all night, as thoughts of them undressed and so nearby eroded his serenity. In 1933, when Director Ernst Röhm and his homosexual coterie were executed, Ernst, sick to his stomach, made a decision.

But his father, holding up one finger and raising his eyebrows over his pale blue eyes, had cautioned him not to resign then. Which was surprising. For stolid old Prussian families like the vom Raths did not approve of bloodbaths; they whispered among themselves how clowns had taken over the country. "If the National Socialists do well," his father pronounced, "Party membership will look good for you."

"I was right, wasn't I?" decreed the senior vom Rath after examining his son's résumé. He put down his glass of schnapps so resolutely that it made a resounding crack on the glass desktop. He rose and marched up the stairs, turning off the lights on each landing and leaving Ernst in the dark in the library.

That night, after Ernst walked up the carpeted steps, past the portraits, he stood in front of his mirror and swiveled this way and that as his brothers, together, like conspirators, slept across the hall. He tried combing his hair over his forehead. He sucked in his stomach and turned sideways. But the sad man in the mirror had hair that was vaguely blond and eyes that were blue and watery; his body looked waterlogged. If he smiled encouragement, no one detected the begging or protective irony behind the gesture. The world (and the mirror) pronounced Ernst vom Rath a failure. And he took this judgment as he took everything else—to heart, secretly.

At the El Dorado, Ernst hovered at the door. He walked toward it but turned back. He did not dare. What if someone from work saw him?

He paced a bit, then went across the street and looked about. At the cafe he sat at one of the round outdoor tables and ordered a drink. He sipped it, looking about discreetly.

A man at another table eyed him.

It looked like the man might come over. Ernst turned his head and realized that such signals were all around him. A thousand eyes, all weighing, evaluating. This was too much like what had happened in India. He refused to meet the audacious dark eyes of a well-dressed white-haired man who kept glancing Ernst's way and fidgeting pointedly. Ernst had to leave. But the boy . . .

If someone from work walked by, Ernst could say he was enjoying the night. He sat back, inspected his own watch, and looked up and down the street as if he were expecting somebody. The waiter, a young man with a goatee, in dark pants and a white shirt, came up again and again to check on him. Ernst allowed himself one more glass.

Fifteen minutes seemed an eternity. Then, hearing a gust of dance music, he looked up. The Jew boy stood in front of the dance hall, looking up and down the street.

He doesn't see me yet.

Herschel started across the street.

Now he does.

The boy stopped. The muscles in his jaw twitched.

Ernst stood and pulled out a chair. "Hello. Care to join me?"

He came up, breathless. The waiter appeared.

"Un jus d'orange," he said quietly. And Ernst held out his glass for a refill.

They sat.

The German sipped his wine. They looked into each other's eyes as if looking for some lost thing. "I saw you at the consulate," Ernst said.

Herschel nodded. Men at the other tables stared.

That made Ernst nervous. "I have something to tell you. Want to walk along with me?"

"Su-ure."

"I'll go first and then you follow."

He paid and left a tip; the waiter came to take the empty glass away, and Herschel stood and stretched; he followed Ernst around the corner.

Watching the boy walk over, Ernst remembered his last cycling trip—how he had stopped for a drink offered by a tall, strapping shirtless farm boy with blue eyes and dazzling white teeth. As he handed over a cup, the fellow wiped his face with the back of his hand. Ernst had longed to wheel his bicycle along the rutted dirt path to the farmhouse. There, bronzed, blond Dolph or Gustavus or whatever his name was would step from his clothes. When he touched the boy's chest, Ernst would have felt the sun's exuberant heat.

Now he wanted to be in control, to have this dark boy want him. Ernst asked, "Can you come with me?"

Herschel too was breathing shallowly. He nodded. They walked along till Ernst saw a dark doorway and pushed him in. Their lips met; they started clawing each other.

"Wait!" Ernst cried out in a sob and darted into a badly lit doorway that had a hotel sign overhead.

Herschel watched Ernst's shadow through a frosted glass window until he emerged, waving a key.

A moment later Herschel followed up some steps.

He found himself in a dim hall with doors to the right and left. Halfway down the corridor, a door opened.

Ernst waved him in.

Herschel entered; Ernst threw the bolt and turned to face the boy. For a second nothing happened. Then they went at each other in a rush, like fighters, angry at the clumsy resistance of their clothed bodies.

Ernst fell back and dropped to his knees. He flung his arms around the boy's waist and looked up at Herschel, who pursed his lips and raised a shoulder provocatively.

Ernst got up and slowly led the boy to the sway-backed bed. Herschel followed, knowing how it would be.

But the German got control of himself. He inhaled deeply and stroked Herschel's face. "Come. Sit."

Ernst stared down at him. "Sorry," he began, "for being so fast."

Herschel willed him to be brutal, take command, force him. When he didn't, the boy sighed and turned away.

"What is it?"

Herschel pulled Ernst down. He ground his hips against the German, but the older man just gave him a quick kiss and then pulled back, patting his hair away from his forehead.

Herschel rolled away and, sighing, got up.

"Please! I, I'm—Stay for a minute."

"No! Let me go!"

"Lower your voice! Someone might hear!"

"Stop!"

"Shhh." Ernst put his hand over Herschel's mouth; Herschel bit him.

Ernst yelped. And heat rose in him. He thrust the boy down on the bed, pinning his wrists.

"Yes!" Herschel went limp, delirious. Ernst felt the change, slipped his hand under the boy, and pulled him closer. "So this is what you want?"

"I need!" Herschel called out as the room spun. "Hit me!" But there was only the violence of his feelings.

The man was overcome. He pulled at his clothes; Herschel struggled out of his trousers; Ernst tugged his shirt over his head. Ernst threw his weight on the boy. They kissed, moving their mouths over each other's skin. In an instant they were at a crisis, a cliff, ready to tumble, but Ernst slowed. He stroked Herschel's forehead and looked into his eyes. In the background above him, Herschel sensed walls and ceiling vanishing.

Ernst lifted, and Herschel bit his lip. They hung weightless, outside time, beyond their bodies.

Ernst nodded as they began moving to each other as if one was on the ground, pushing someone in a swing. They breached time and space and all bonds of need.

After six months of waiting back home for his next assignment, Ernst vom Rath learned where his new posting would be.

"India!" his brothers shouted and started to laugh.

"An important part of the world," his father countered quickly, and Ernst blushed, aware of his mother's polite dismay and his two brothers' pity. There was no doubt: India, with its darker races and non-Aryan culture, meant exile, defeat. But in a strange way Ernst vom Rath had felt relief. At least he would not have to keep up a facade and try to fool anybody. And, as if everyone knew this, no one tried to dissuade him from leaving right away, even though it did not appear that he was needed, even at the bottom of the world, immediately.

He was shocked upon arrival on the subcontinent; the heat was sweltering and the air assaulted him, so thick that it had a taste. Everything was tarnished and used up, even the metallic air he was somehow expected to breathe.

He despaired of finding a clean white room or one that matched the meanings of "clean" and "white" in his vocabulary. His clothes clung to him. Like a slug, he left a trail in the humid heat, a slick slime on the sweating concrete.

Every morning he went dutifully through the shimmer and stench to work in the embassy. He marched along in dress whites, hatted in the glare, a handkerchief over his mouth, going early and leaving late in the scented, lilac-colored evening.

But like the flaking plaster that he found in the arched rooms of Government House, Ernst's own invulnerability caved in. Mornings were splendid, with the elephants in procession and the great green prehistoric leaves of the bushes in the garden. He stirred; the place aroused in him an almost erotic longing. After six weeks he did not tie his tie so expertly; he rested in bed, sweating, and did not get up so early. He took his time in the market, dawdled on verandas during cocktails, grinned, and began to joyfully greet the fierce heat and the place's sinister fecundity. His sweat trickling down his chest aroused him.

Looking at the long-legged German doctor on the embassy staff, Ernst gave in to rabid daylight dreams. The doctor's lean torso, and his careless movements as he played tennis, made Ernst want to shout, "Thank God for beauty!" He imagined walking down the street wearing nothing. His eyes furtively noticed flesh everywhere; men were all around him, in the embassy, the barracks, the streets—men looking, talking, touching other men on their arms, on the back of their necks. They were vivid as peacocks, and there were also elegant smiling brown boys with dark hair and bodies. He felt their gazes on him like the brush of silk.

Boys watched on the streets and in parks when he got out of a rickshaw; they followed him into shops, but the proprietors ejected them. When Ernst was back on the street, a crowd of boys awaited; each took his hands and pulled. "Me, mister, me!" they shrieked in their singsong pidgin, apparently confusing him with someone from England. Like beggars, they put their hands in his pocket and groped. (Ernst found their streetwise ways appalling.)

Crying, panicking (how do they know? he wondered), Ernst beat them off, pushed away their nut-hard bodies. Shopkeepers yelled and shooed in high-pitched voices. Ernst pulled out his handkerchief, mopped his forehead, and bit his lip to keep from crying.

On one dazzling white-hot day the walls and streets glowed; it was too bright to see. A boy fell alongside Ernst and reached into his trousers. The boy looked up. Ernst nodded and the boy babbled and Ernst stared into golden eyes; it was like being eye to eye with a snake.

The boy pulled him through a doorway.

Other men and boys, most of them dark, were in there. Dark flesh of dark boys with lighter palms wound around him.

Suddenly, he was stark white; he had to cover himself with darkness, hard slim dark male bodies. He bucked and swayed, threw back his head, and wanted to shout, "I am a rutting beast." But then he was lost again, back in the heat.

And he was trapped in his shameful body, the one that was soft and white and wet like a slug's. Boys had entwined him like vines, lewd as lascivious temple carvings. He lifted one's head from his lap. The boy held out a hand for money.

Ernst dressed and ran; he threw up in the street.

After work, at home in the hot late afternoon and cooling evening, he tried to read and write letters, but the desire came back. If his mind had been silent before, it was now filled with the sound of ten thousand flies buzzing. When the sound got louder, Ernst went back to the market and visited a boy named Jamahl or something like that. Jamahl was dark, burnished. He had a winning look, a handsome face, eloquent slow eyes, and ivory white teeth. Jamahl's smile was wisdom revealed.

Every night for weeks, the German stumbled home, whistling under his breath, sated and graced, at peace. All other times—at work, at home—he put on his mask, the face of the Ernst he had once been. India was lit by a different sun, and he was no longer one of his family. He had an idea that it was possible to be happy.

One night he walked home late, alone in the streets he was beginning to love. Not till he reached his quarters at three in the morning and reached for his billfold did he realize it was missing.

He cried and stopped. Maybe he had not taken it.

Though he knew he had, he searched his room. He turned over everything. Then desperation arrived with its own quiet authority. He undressed and bathed, then straightened up his quarters, which he had ravaged searching for his wallet.

He lay down and looked up. His unblinking eyes saw the fan, the cracks in the ceiling. He saw the future unfold on that screen: Jamahl, or his pimp, would appear and demand politely to see him. And him only. "I have secrets," he would say.

If Ernst paid, he'd be allowed back in like old opium addicts with sunken eyes and yellow teeth returning to their den. And if he would not pay, they would ruin him with blackmail. This he knew. How could it be happening to someone who had done so well in school, had attended the opera in Paris, and came from a distinguished family? His mother would die; he'd be banned from his family.

By six the sun was up, its heavy yellow light breaking like a yoke on the walls. He entered the embassy with the demeanor of someone about to face a firing squad.

The next three days passed in a fevered dream.

He entered his office on the fourth day and saw his leather billfold lying face-up on his desk, empty and accusing. He approached the guard in the hallway.

"You found this?"

"Some little beggar brought it in," the man answered, avoiding his eyes.

Ernst's knees weakened.

"Did he speak to you?"

"No, sir. It was Security." He pointed, and Ernst went downstairs, where the rooms on the eastern side of the building were constantly busy. Directly under a ceiling fan sat a fat florid man with a big nose, many chins, and an old-fashioned walrus moustache. Sweat made continent-shaped stains in his khakis, which stuck to him. Pictures of his wife and children sat on the desk in discolored celluloid frames.

Ernst showed him the wallet. "Someone brought this in?"

Schloss wiped his prodigious moustache and nodded. "You should have told us it was stolen."

"I didn't realize . . . I thought I misplaced it. I . . . didn't suspect anybody."

Schloss made a stern face, as if he could not approve of such vagueness. "A little beggar had it; we got an interpreter to explain what the creature was saying. Said he did not take it or want anything—said he had found it where you left it, at his house! Just did not want you to worry!" He looked at Ernst. "Have you ever heard such a thing!"

He shook his head.

"We knew he was playing some sort of game. We do not allow that here under my regime."

Ernst stood, dreading what was to come. And Schloss rewarded him.

"I had him beaten," Schloss volunteered. "For stealing; there was blood in his eyes when we threw him into the street."

Ernst moved his lips. How lovely Jamahl was. How sickening. He turned, but Schloss called after him. "He cried and cried, kept saying he did not want you to think he had stolen it. Where were you? Where were you? he kept crying."

"Imagine," Ernst said. "Excuse me."

He went to a sink and bathed his face and darted to

a stall when someone came in. He ran from others in the hall, even turning into a closet once, whenever he saw someone from Security approach. Everyone had to know, everyone had to be laughing.

He stopped going out, kept the rattan blinds down, avoided the light, and worried about a rash between his legs that would not heal.

He scented his handkerchief against the stench of the heat and no longer walked, taking instead a bicycle rickshaw to and from work. The heat tightened its vise on him; the insects taunted; beauty stung. The rash got worse. At night he examined the area above his waist with his pants on and then donned a shirt to examine below.

The rash spread. One hot day he fainted in a breezeway.

At the hospital the handsome blond doctor from the tennis courts examined him with cool dry powdered hands. "One of the worst heat rashes I've seen."

"Heat?"

"Of course," the god answered. "And you fainted. You're dehydrated. From dysentery."

"Is that all?"

With a quizzical smile the doctor shook his head. "When I listened to your lungs, I thought I . . . The left—we'll do tests, but it's a touch of tuberculosis, I think."

"What does that mean?"

The doctor looked down. His fair hair, like a rime of frost against tanned skin, made Ernst weak. The doctor's hands were elegant and lean, the fingers tapered, nails manicured.

Save me; love me.

"It's back to civilization for you. You're lucky it's not worse. One discovers such vileness in dark countries."

In India, the minister's pen wrote, *he caught tuberculosis. He suffered for his country.*

Back home after the boat trip, Ernst, thin and weak, was sent to recover at St. Blasien's Sanitorium in the Black Forest. Weeks went by. He relished the monklike quiet, the white sheets, the nurses pushing carts of food and medicines on quiet rubber wheels. He lay on the chaise lounge in pajamas and a robe, under a blanket or sheet. He ate, lay down for naps, and drifted dreamlessly to sleep.

The nurses' whispers and warm soft breezes wafted through the screens. All he had to do was eat and read and wander the paths that went from the dark green lawns into the scented darker green of the trees. He was hemmed in by the low gray stone wall, protected from the frenzy of the world, its frets, desires, and activities. Just reading about them in the crackling newspaper upset him.

"I've been wondering," he wrote on a postcard home. "I want to go back to university. Teach. It may be that foreign service is not for me."

He put his pen down and, licking the stamp, imagined the card arriving; Frida, the maid, would hand it over to his tall gray-haired mother; she would recognize the handwriting but would wait for her husband to read it to her that evening. What a scene there would be.

Ernst tore up the card; looking about, he swiftly pocketed all the pieces, wetting his finger to pick up a fallen shred.

The next day, on another piece of paper, he wrote, "I am scared." When a nurse came up to check on him, he pretended to be writing a letter.

"To your girlfriend?"

Ernst agreed.

"I want to be loved; I want to be free." He spoke the words to the air, to the trees. But they whispered nothing back. Sitting in the garden, he watched a young tanned soldier kiss a nurse and slip his hand into her starched white blouse. She parted her moist lips. Ernst jumped up and ran, his heart beating, till he stopped against the wrinkled trunk of a spruce. The day's heat was at its zenith. I am at my peak, he thought, hitting his head against the bark. And no one will ever know it. No one will ever know me. He had grown lean in the hospital—like a greyhound, curved and panting. He could not draw or play music or sing, yet his soul soared when he read and watched and listened. He was capable of great things.

But who knew? Who cared? Outside there was no one. He had to stay here. But the police, that is how he thought of the doctors and nurses now, kept insisting. For his country, for the great age, the Reich, he should attend craft classes and do his deep breathing.

He fell in with the other patients on the lawn for calisthenics in the morning and helped move trestle tables in the dining hall and set up the chairs for evening movies. They watched flickering newsreels of the shouting Führer and his limping Goebbels at massive torchlit rallies. Ernst's heart sank as he sat, aware that he was as doomed as the men in dresses in dance halls in Berlin. They pretended to sing songs as disks spun on a gramophone; now he too mouthed and gave lip service. "Hitler this; Hitler that; the past, the future, Germany." Then he excused himself and walked back in the moonlight, breathing in the soft air, dreaming.

He was summoned to the chief physician's office one flawless early winter morning and shown his x-ray. There was no heart or soul to be seen, but his lungs showed clear.

For his last evening he joined his parents, who had come in the car for him. At a nearby mountain inn their waiter slowly filled tall champagne flutes, and his mother, restrained and gray and serene, kissed him. Father raised his glass. "Good news. You'll go to Berlin for a briefing."

"And after?" He put down his glass.

"Like I told you: Your party membership has done you good. It's back to . . ."

Ernst trembled at the whiteness of India, the boys in the streets.

"Paris!" His father winked.

"Congratulations," his mother smiled, breaking her formality. "Your brothers are so proud of you."

Amazed, Ernst thought, was more likely. He reached for his champagne. They touched their flutes together, making the glasses sing.

In Paris he took on extra duties; he freed up his colleagues. Thanks to Ernst, they could drink in cafes by the Seine or take weekends in the country. At night he left long after everyone else had.

He volunteered for extra hours, the minister Joseph Goebbels noted on a sheet of stationery as he drafted Ernst's obituary. *He often came in early, making him the most senior staff on duty.*

"That's when something important may happen to you," his father wrote encouragingly.

But when day expired like a sigh and a violet light announced the night, Ernst rose to peer from his window at the silhouettes of buildings and trees against a mauve background of evening. "Good night," the porter called.

Outside, sometimes Ernst had a hope, a feeling. That things could change. That it was not too late. He thrilled at the thought on the night that he took the mail to the consulate that had been misdirected to the embassy.

Ernst woke, sat up, and the room swung into focus. What had just happened? The boy. Where was he?

In the middle of the room stood an apparition.

Herschel moved about, naked.

He had Ernst's trousers in his hand and was going through the pockets. He pulled out a wallet but stopped. The moonlight bleached the room bone white. He looked at his fingers as if acid burned them.

"What are you doing?"

The boy spun around. "Nothing." He dropped the trousers and the wallet. "I was just looking for a cigarette!"

"Oh, no, you weren't. Come here," Ernst demanded.

"But," the boy said, "I have to leave."

"No. Come here."

Herschel came over and sat on the edge of the bed; he drew up his knees. Ernst blew on his shoulder and let his fingers drift down the boy's flesh; the sensation sizzled. He touched the attenuated hollow in Herschel's thigh, like the indentation of a knife blade. "Lovely."

Herschel watched as the man fell to his knees. The earth gave way, as he slipped through the veil, into a wash of warm emotion, disembodied. It was wonderful, like being born or entering a warm pool, flowing out of his body.

Ernst looked up, and Herschel, high on the bed, felt wise, omniscient. He smiled benignly as Ernst crawled into his lap and fell asleep. For a long time he sat stroking Ernst's temple; he forgave everything. But then a ticking entered the boy's consciousness. He shifted the slumbering man, squeezed out from under him. He dressed and went deftly through the clothes on the floor.

He turned back to the bed to look at Ernst one more time.

Ernst was watching. His eyes in the moonlight were milky, eerie.

Herschel turned to the door, swirling the moonlight like mist.

"Stop—please! I want to see you again. How can I find you?"

Herschel knew it was impossible. As their eyes locked, Herschel thought, I am always lying. "Twenty-three Richard Lenoir."

He was out in the hallway in an instant. Ernst saw him toss something back through the door. He was still not dressed, but he did not care about the maid who stared. Ernst went to the door, bent, and found it.

He closed the door; he leaned against the frame and put his wallet to his lips.

Aunt Chawa looked up, a heel of bread and some cheese in her hand.

"You're in late." Her eyes searched his. He looked away, afraid he'd break out smiling. "Nathan and I went to the films."

"What did you see?"

"You wouldn't have liked it." He usually saw detective films. She liked love stories.

"Good night," he called out. He washed quickly. He sat on the edge of his bed in the moonlight.

In Berlin the minister put down his pen and looked at the pages of his handwriting in front of him. Within a few days it would be true.

The sun warmed Paris that next morning and woke Herschel Grynszpan.

"Stupid," he murmured to the mirror. His lips were chapped and red rode over the tender flesh. He ran his finger over the tingling. In the kitchen Uncle Abraham glanced at his watch and told him he was lazy. He reached out to cuff him. But Herschel ducked away. Mean old man, he thought; he should leave. Instead of thinking of home, however, he was reliving last night. He thought of it all morning, measuring the bolts of fabrics, cutting at the chalk lines that Uncle had drawn. Maybe he could go back to the hotel with the German!

At lunch he went out on the street and looked up at the sun and clouds. Why did trees bloom? Why did the earth bring forth beauty? He spent the afternoon in his room, lying on his bed, watching the dust motes dance in the light that poured in.

At supper Chawa put noodles and chicken on his plate. But Herschel would not, could not, eat, and

Chawa bit her lip. He mumbled excuses and said he had friends to see.

When he got to the cafe, he saw Nathan. Herschel pulled up a chair and nodded but did not speak. He leaned against the wall, smoked, and watched the El Dorado's doorway. The moon rose, and, like a tide, light rushed in. There were sudden shadows under objects, and the known world was thrown into relief. Herschel jerked involuntarily as a dog will in sleep. He stroked up and down his arm. When the moon hung bone white above the trees, he got up.

"Tomorrow," he told Nathan. Hands in his pockets, he moved toward home.

It was a dream. The German seemed out of time in his suit and tidy blond looks. He looked pasted on the background, like an item in a collage. But he was three-dimensional.

Ernst strolled up, smiling. His pale blue eyes sparkled, his thin bland face almost handsome. Herschel looked him over, then at the malevolent, grim building.

"Twenty-three Richard Lenoir," Ernst explained, showing his teeth. "I didn't know which apartment, just stood on the street, wondering."

His eyes moved all over the boy.

Two fox-faced women passed and looked askance from under their kerchiefs.

"That's it, sir. Just like I said, you can find your way from here."

The women moved on.

Ernst looked at him in anguish.

"You don't want to see me."

"I do! but . . ." He nodded at the women, who now looked back. "They know my aunt."

Herschel stopped.

"I'll go," Ernst volunteered.

But Herschel cried, "No."

They ran down the street.

They slowed down to walk along under trees laced with moonlight. They spoke. After a while they decided: The hotel they had gone to the night before was called the Istanbul, they saw. In the room, the same, number twenty, trapezoids of light crossed the bed and went up the walls, some bending backward on the ceiling, like a crazy modernist painting.

They undressed as the light made angles on their naked bodies. They lay in the bed, and light lifted them as if in a boat. An apotheosis.

It was not like India. And it was not day, not night but a world incandescent with significance. And the room, the walls, the dirty windows, and their flesh too, all were washed in the pearl essence, like a shell, opalescent.

The clerk at the Hotel Istanbul heard the door close. Then the bed springs complaining. After a furious bout, peace.

An hour later feet made sounds on the ceiling. The older, blond one came in to return the key. He stood out on the street.

Someone came down the steps then. A dark wraith-like boy. They looked at each other, did not touch, did not speak. Soundlessly, they moved off in opposite directions, each one looking back at the other. Other customers came in, and he handed a man and woman a key.

That was how it should be. But the blond man—he spoke French with an accent—said he would want the room again the next night. He had tipped well but still. Men. Disgusting.

In Berlin Propaganda Minister Joseph Goebbels took a break in his research. Odd, but in the summer of 1938 vom Rath's behavior had changed, his personnel records showed; he did not stay late anymore or come in early. He took days off and was written up twice, actually. His superior, Jorns, noted something about an illicit affair. What did it mean? Could he have had a love affair with Mademoiselle Taulin, his tutor?

It would look good—to have a Frenchwoman mourning the hero, along with all of Germany.

Each night Ernst and Herschel met at the hotel, one waiting for the other on the street, almost not daring to look each other in the eye, until they could be upstairs, behind the door.

After a while, they got over their nervousness. As spring advanced, they grew more confident. The ease, the desire to be together, thinking of each other all day, waiting for the evening, revealed that what was between them would not evaporate.

Nothing, no doubt or fear or even duty, could intervene. Believing, invincible, they went on meeting, evening after evening.

And then leaving.

One o'clock in the morning. No breeze relieved the hot, deserted streets. The boy twirled; he floated, citizen—no, ruler—of his own country. Like smoke, he rose in the Maison Albert's stairway. But the hall light was on, and he heard voices.

Aunt Chawa, Uncle Abraham, and Uncle Solomon fell silent. On the threshold of the dining room, Herschel could not, would not, enter their dimension. But they waved him in.

"This came today," Aunt Chawa said; her powdered cheeks showed tear streaks. Uncle Abraham lifted the long envelope with its official-looking seal. Herschel's heart lurched. He opened it but could not focus.

"What does it mean?"

Uncle Abraham swallowed. "I called on the Jewish Committee. But they could do nothing. It's too late. It's an expulsion order."

Herschel looked blank.

"You'll be deported."

"Deported?"

"Your papers are still not right. You have to leave France."

"When?"

"Within a week."

He almost laughed—"I won't!"

"You will do as I—"

"NO! I won't!"

Uncle Abraham rose, but Chawa said sharply, "Let's not argue," and then softened her voice, adding, "please."

Abraham sat down. Chawa twisted a hand around her fist.

Uncle Solomon broke in. "For a change, you might want to visit Hanover. Of course, you'd have to sneak back, like you did, coming in—"

"Quiet," Chawa insisted, "he's staying." She smiled at him tenderly—and Herschel nodded; he kissed her powdered cheek. "We have to think of something."

"Yes!" the boy agreed.

He looked at them. Uncle Solomon chewed his lip. Uncle Abraham's face was stern, eyes angry. Herschel went to get a drink.

In the kitchen he heard Solomon and Abraham whispering. "We'll be in trouble if they find him here."

They want me to be noble. He put the glass down. To volunteer.

"I have an idea," he said, coming back. I'm just a boy.

"I know someone who might help me." Would he?

"Jewish?" Aunt Chawa asked.

"Of course."

"Who?" asked Uncle Abraham, suspicious.

"A man. I was just with him, talking about these things."

"What's his name?"

"Roth," Herschel answered.

"I made a dress once," Abraham smiled, "for a Roth wedding. They loved it. I bet it's the same family!"

Herschel nodded. If that was what he wanted to believe . . . He left the room grandly. "Goodness," Chawa said, staring proudly at his back. "What a man he's becoming."

He smiled to himself as he undressed and got into bed, into crisp, clean sheets. Maybe they could go to an inn, as Ernst promised, in the country. As dreams merged with the real (he did have a permit; it was all a misunderstanding; Ernst was smiling at him), a knock shattered it.

"What?"

"Your papers," Chawa whispered, "your friend, don't you want to ask him right away if he'll—"

"Go away!"

"Your uncle says you should get up."

No sound.

"For me, please, see to it right away. It's almost morning."

"Oh, all right!"

Didn't they understand? Couldn't they see? He could not pay attention to such foolish things as laws and decrees.

Aunt Chawa served them all a big breakfast of lox, hard rolls, and coffee, but Herschel drank only a small cup. They kept looking at him, and when he got up from the table, they followed. He could feel them all staring down from the window as he went down the street.

It's not my fault, he thought, looking up. Chawa waved; Herschel turned away.

At the Tuileries he sat on a bench, tossing his hair; he'd make them wait all day. He watched old men read papers and children play near their nurses.

When he returned, the summer sun had peaked. Uncle looked up from his sewing machine, through his half glasses.

"Nu?" he asked.

"It's done. My friend said he will cancel the expulsion order while we wait for my visa." He looked at his nails, feigned boredom, and sighed expansively.

Uncle Abraham looked dumbfounded. "Are you sure?"

But Chawa was already hugging him, crying, "Mazel tov! We'll do it now—we'll find a new apartment with a room of your own!" She looked at her husband, who watched the boy. Abraham did not look pleased.

At eight Herschel left the Maison Albert. He ran past buildings, people, and automobiles into the heady timelessness of evening. In the hotel he undressed.

His heart rose like a fountain when Ernst came in. Ernst's movements exuded reason—he put down his briefcase, took off and folded his jacket methodically, as if there were rules and regulations to govern everything. Herschel went to him.

"Do you want something?"

"Yes."

Ernst smiled back, fumbling at buttons. "And I do too."

"Not that!" But Ernst reached for him as he tugged down his trousers. Herschel wanted to speak. But Ernst turned him around and kissed behind his ear.

"I—" Ernst's mouth slid like a snail over his shoulder. His lips were stretched as if in agony. "I—" Herschel lifted his head, throwing it back, as if letting his hair fly free at the seashore. Ernst held onto him as Herschel bent his arms backward around Ernst's neck. Ernst growled low in his throat and nuzzled Herschel's ear, which made the boy writhe; they were back in their transcendent sphere.

Herschel woke first. Gently, he moved his finger like a skier down the white slopes of his lover's body. Let the newspapers rail and Uncle and Aunt wail; all that mattered was right here. But still. There was that letter

Uncle had shown him. Herschel caught Ernst's eye as he woke.

"What is it?" Ernst asked.

Herschel made a face, swallowed. He had to speak. But nothing would come out.

"What is it? Tell me."

Herschel shook his head, whispered hotly in Ernst's ear.

The next night as he lay on his stomach and Ernst sat, Herschel sank his chin into Ernst's lap. "I have to ask you something."

Ernst grinned, "Wait! I need a few minutes to get my strength up."

"No, it's not that."

"What?"

His voice trembled as the fear came up like mist. "It's serious."

Ernst jerked upright, looking worried. "Is it something I did?"

"No! It's just . . . I need a favor."

"Oh." He sounded like a balloon deflating. Just that morning the staff had been warned in one of the weekly meetings. They had sat through a lecture and film of swarming rats that turned into crook-nosed Jews, running down gangplanks of ships. Jews would snatch at and entangle you. Oh, he pleaded to himself, to God, to the room. Don't let him ask me for anything illegal, please.

"A visa."

It was like a slap. He gasped.

Which startled Herschel. "That's what I need."

Silence—and then with a voice squeaky with suspicion and fear, Ernst continued. "For whom? You?"

Herschel saw his panic. "No. Not for me."

"Who?"

He got out of bed. "A friend!"

"What KIND of friend?"

"A Jewish friend!" he answered, and Ernst stopped. Herschel, nude, was walking around the room. "A cousin of mine!"

Ernst nodded, smiled bravely, while the pulse in his forehead throbbed. He heard himself speak. "Tell me."

"A neighbor of my aunt's slipped over the border, without German papers—and no money for a visa—and now since she didn't leave officially, she can't return . . . and her family . . ."

Ernst seemed to wither, shrink. Herschel felt his heart constrict. And then he thought of Aunt Chawa and Uncle Abraham. They had brought up these things. They're trying to break us up, he thought angrily.

Ernst swallowed.

"No!" Herschel spun around to face Ernst. "Forget it!"

Ernst looked up gratefully. "Oh, Herschel. I love you," he said.

Herschel burst into tears and Ernst grabbed him. They held to each other as if just snatched from disaster. For minutes there was no peripheral vision, no memory, no uncle and aunt, no Jews, no Germany. The world was as blurred as landscape from a train window. Only what happened between them in their room was real.

But later, in the Maison Albert, when Herschel tried to recall their evening together, it was hollow. Here the rules of Abraham and Chawa and France and Germany were as tangible as the grit in the air that made your eyes weep. Here what went on in that hotel room could not be believed. Here he could not stop the dread that was a pit in his stomach and dampness under his arms.

Yet all he had to do was leave and go back to the hotel and see Ernst. How light he was—his almost straight nose, flat cheeks, fair brows and lashes; his eyes the blue of old china that had faded into its own glaze, subsumed its own glory. When they closed the door, the world disappeared.

Their evenings burned like the cafe lights in the trees they sat under. They were strung one to another, glowing luminously. They smiled, did not speak, as the waiter brought them drinks.

It felt delicious, delaying, putting off the moment that they would, like fire and powder, kiss and consume and extinguish each need. Thinking of it, they'd get up at the same moment, as if they had been sharing identical thoughts, had the same idea. The waiter would watch them vanish down the street.

In bed, as moonlight and night made bars across their bodies, they laughed, refusing to heed the auguries in the rustle of the leaves. Ernst passed his tongue over his teeth; he lay like a sultan in luxury, running his hand through Herschel's dark hair. Listening to the laughter from the cafe below, and its obscene hurdy-gurdy, the boy sucked Ernst's fingertips greedily.

In the heat Ernst got up to get a glass and filled it from the sink. He stood naked in the moonlight.

"What are you thinking?" Herschel asked, as he drowsed in the sheets.

"About you."

"Me?"

"Where were you before we met?" He came up to the boy and nibbled his ear. "What did you do?"

Herschel's eyes brightened. This was his chance—to tell all, his past, his coming here. How dramatic and noble he'd appear. Ernst would see his suffering. Then he would save him, get him papers, be moved to tears.

He got up.

"What is it?"

Herschel looked perplexed, as if he could not speak.

Like a threat, the past hung over him and he wanted to flee it—escape the sad, unhappy, cowering creature he'd been back in Germany. But if he told Ernst about that Herschel, I'll be him again, he thought.

He went back to the bed and pulled Ernst down on top of him.

But Ernst persisted, riddling him with questions the next night. "Tell me about your past, please." He rattled off his own, the places he had gone to school: Berlin, Frankfurt, Königsberg.

"I never fit in; I didn't want a career," he confessed and laughed. "My father; my family! They're so stiff, so formal!" He looked at Herschel, who fell back, biting his ragged nails, his dark eyes worried. Could he do that?

"Please." Ernst pressed the boy. "Tell me more, about your family back home, not just your aunt and uncle here."

"I can't!" Herschel gasped. "We're too different."

"But we mesh," Ernst coaxed, bringing him back to bed.

"My family," said Herschel, closing his eyes. "They'll stop." Ernst moved. "Don't stop."

"I'll take care of you." Herschel twisted, arched and lifted, licked his lips. "I . . . I . . . I . . . want . . ."

The flesh was gone, the veil torn.

"Not family," he whimpered through clenched teeth.

Their need grew with the heat. Their happiness could fill hemispheres as they dallied in the Bois, on banks of green dappled by sun and shadow. They sat for hours by the river, watching barges pass. They ate long loafs of bread and drank a bottle of red wine that seemed to make Herschel sad. Later, in a field they lay together face up, watching the clouds puff up and disappear like dandelions in a breeze. Under Ernst's jacket, spread on the grass between them, they held hands; they sighed with happiness and satisfaction as the wind soughed through the branches. Like butterflies, spots of sun danced here and there on them.

They dozed. And then they got up and walked. Ernst looked about; no one was coming, so he held out his hand. Herschel grabbed it. For a while they walked, toward the torn bits of music they could barely hear.

A young priest loomed ahead; they dropped hands quickly.

Other picnickers came out on the long graveled paths that were bordered by tall waving trees; Herschel and Ernst followed the crowd. They stopped at a bandstand where musicians were gathering and tuning.

Old couples sat on wooden chairs, while younger men and women, some common and poor, others well groomed, lay down on blankets, coats off, sprawling against each other. Ernst and Herschel sat quietly among the flowers, now glowing like embers in the pale lavender of coming night. No one objected as Herschel and Ernst joined the universe, the history of that evening.

The music began. The brasses were fate, violins the stream, the woodwinds premonitions pierced with auguries. As the fugue inverted, their lives interlocked, and, under Ernst's jacket, their fingers linked.

Herschel began to fear the music's end, the stars' fading. Ernst looked back at him and squeezed the boy's hand more tightly.

"You know," Herschel thought.

Ernst's eyes misted; he nodded slowly.

In the dark they looked at each other, releasing their grip only when the music ceased and the audience leaped to its feet, applauding; Herschel and Ernst did too. As the audience broke up, both felt the evanescence, the poignancy of the dying sounds. They could not speak in the ride back in the taxi.

And in their room they were silent still, clinging to each other, not wanting to acknowledge the church bells insisting that they leave. Laughter from the cafe slowed.

In the sudden silence, and the sweeping up of smashed glasses, they rose.

They went to the window and looked at the city, poured out in moonlight in front of them; Ernst saw names carved in the soft sill and went to find his trousers; he took a small knife from his pocket and dug diligently.

The light kept them from speaking as it filled the hollows that Ernst cut; curls and tendrils of wood fell to the floor. The light seemed to waver like water, like mercury.

Herschel traced his finger in the fresh hollows, *HG & EvR*.

"I have an idea," Ernst whispered before leaving.

"I'm giving him French lessons," Ernst explained that next night, pushing Herschel toward his landlady. Madame LaRoche, vast and amiable, spent most of the day in a small chair by the doorway. She nodded her crimped curls and smiled from the network of crushed veins in her happy ovoid face.

"If you don't mind, we'll work most evenings." Ernst presented her with a small flask of brandy. She blushed as she pocketed it.

The boy paused, smiled, looked uncertain as they went in. Ernst watched to see whether Herschel would like his rooms and especially how Ernst had decorated them with posters and reproductions of great paintings. There was even a watercolor sylvan scene he had done as a boy back in Germany.

Herschel fell silent, as if in a museum or a place too exalted for him, relaxing only when Ernst came from behind and squeezed him. After they made love, Ernst took him again through the rooms and showed him his things, explaining what they meant and where they had come from.

When Herschel left (Ernst walked him down past Madame LaRoche), Ernst went back upstairs, content; it was almost as if he had introduced Herschel to his family.

The next night Herschel let himself in with the key that Ernst had given him. He went over to the oval silver-framed photographs of a man and a woman and two young men. He waited like an actor in a play that would begin when Ernst entered. There was room to breathe, to be, believe. He could listen to the radio, look out the window, remember the night before, expect things. But he just sat waiting, imagining how one day he might not feel a stranger here.

He was sitting in the front room, with the picture of the stiff man and the woman in his hand, when he heard a key in the door.

Ernst came up and hugged him.

"What have you there?" he asked, grabbing what was in the boy's hands. "Is it—?"

He thought it might have been a present for him.

Herschel handed it over guiltily.

"Oh, I see."

Herschel said nothing.

"It's my parents." Ernst tilted it to the light, to get the glare off the glass and stared at the prim woman, her hair tightly coiffed and her lips pinched. The man was clean shaven, fiercely so, with a very serious look and a military bearing. He put it back on the shelf and then took down the photo of his two younger brothers. He handed it to Herschel as if he were surrendering.

Herschel nodded and handed them back. They were very handsome.

After that they found it hard to speak. Ernst turned to him.

"Do you have any photographs of your family—back home?"

Herschel felt a sort of queasy fear.

"Please," Ernst encouraged, "tell me about them."

In his mind's eye he saw them.

He got up. He felt the presence of Solly and Berta like some sort of magnetic pull. His mother. His father glaring at him.

He turned to Ernst. "I don't have any family other than my aunt and uncle here."

"Oh, darling," Ernst said as he rushed up, embraced and held him. "Sweetheart. I am so sorry."

After that night Herschel refused to think of them or what was going on back in Germany. Whenever the thought occurred, he got up and started talking or went to the mirror.

"Come here," he called to Ernst then. "Stand next

to me." They looked like a picture, with the mirror's frame around them.

That was the key, more than the one for the door, that unlocked everything. It meant being a denizen of this world. A place where he was not anyone's son or brother but a lover of the man who stood next to him.

It was so easy now that he had cut free from the past and what it demanded of him.

They never spoke of it, but Ernst knew what they were doing. Hershel was sure of it and felt that he had vanquished a rival. Within a few weeks the photographs of Ernst's family disappeared.

No one knew, no one bothered them in their own special atmosphere. It existed between them even when they went out for meals. And into the country for a whole week.

"I'm going to Zionist camp, getting ready for Palestine, maybe," he said when Chawa asked him where he would be. "And that's why I come home late—I train each evening."

Ernst's apartment was home, not the Maison Albert. He hated leaving.

But each night he had to go past Madame LaRoche and return to Chawa and Abraham. It got harder and harder as the days grew shorter and cooler and a chill in the air announced the October mornings. And it was not just that Ernst's building was so warm and bright with heat. Or that outside it seemed the year was dying.

In November it rained.

One afternoon, shivering in the drizzle, Herschel returned to the Maison Albert after delivering a dress Abraham had altered and a suit he had taken in.

Aunt Chawa, bending over a barrel in the front hall, smiled.

"Herschel! We got it!" Spots of color blazed in her cheeks. She jumped, pulling from her face a piece of straw that she mistook for an insect; she spun it from her hand, laughing.

Herschel looked blank.

She tweaked his nose. "The new apartment! The one with the elevator in the lobby." She laughed at his puzzled look. "Remember? Start bundling your stuff up. There's a room there entirely for you!"

"But." He was going to tell her there was no need; he'd move in with Ernst. He'd say it was a friend. He had been so full these past months that he had forgotten that others dreamed too. He kissed her on her cheek; she beamed. He went in whistling—as through a break in the clouds, the afternoon sun poured in, flooding the inside hall. Motes danced in the light like moments, visible written notes of music.

"Finally!" Uncle Abraham's shadow loomed up like an eclipse, darkening the hall as he opened the door. "What took you so long? Here." He handed Herschel two bolts of black crepe. "Take these down to the street. And get your papers."

"Why?"

Abraham sighed. "We have to present them to get an address change with the police."

"Oh!"

He dropped a bolt. "Stupid," Abraham screamed as it rolled down the steps, the fabric, like a dark stain, unwinding.

Herschel winced. There was no color in his face or life in his voice as he faced his attorneys. "I didn't know I would have to show my papers to the police just to move."

"Weren't they correct yet?"

Herschel looked around.

"What?" Vessine-Larue asked, coming up, cupping his large pink ear, as if he had missed something.

"I had written a letter to the American president, and I prayed for the conference at Evian to succeed."

"And?"

Roosevelt never answered. (Herschel had used the address of Ernst's apartment.) And the delegates at the international meeting, discussing the fate of Germany's Jews, did not decide anything.

"I had told my Uncle I had papers to stay. But he found out my lie when we planned to move."

"What!" Abraham roared.

Aunt Chawa sat down so heavily that she clicked her teeth.

"What do you mean?" he sputtered.

"I had to stay to help my family."

"But you told us, your 'friend' intervened. You said you got a reprieve and got a change in your status."

"Abraham," Chawa chided.

But he persisted, "Show them to me."

"I lost—"

"Show me your papers immediately."

"I can't."

Abraham made a quick worried circle; he looked at Herschel and gasped, could not breathe. "So you've been lying to us all this time?"

Herschel nodded. He was going to explain. "My family—"

But Abraham stamped his feet. "Chawa!" His eyes were frenzied, his mouth wet. "He lied about his status. This momzer!" He lurched at Herschel, who darted away. "We'll be punished for harboring him." He raised his hands and face to heaven, as if shouting for the angels to hear. "He's here illegally."

Herschel tried to speak, but Abraham banged his hands together. "He's been lying to us for months, putting us in danger. This is how he repays our kindness!"

"Herschel!" Chawa chimed in. "Why, honey?"

"I'll tell you why—" Abraham interrupted, wheeling around as if to present a deduction to a jury: "To stay here—and not endanger his tuchis—or get off it! You've betrayed your family!"

Herschel opened his mouth.

"We'll be arrested for harboring you; we'll—"

"But," Chawa wailed, "he can't—he's—"

"Uncle Abraham! I DO have a friend; I'm sure he can help. I'll go see him right away."

"Go!" Abraham shouted, face red and swollen, veins popping in his forehead, spittle flying. "Go!" He rushed at Herschel, who dodged into the hall stairway. "And don't come back. Get yourself out of France; the devil take you. We're no longer responsible for you, Herschel Grynszpan!"

"No," Chawa called out, reaching for Herschel.

"Stop it." Abraham pulled her back. He continued to yell down the stairwell, as doors opened and people looked up. "Get out of here!"

Those watching below pulled in their heads; Herschel scrambled as Abraham picked up a plate from the barrel and hurled it. It crashed in a crescendo, echoing.

Another plate landed with a blood-curdling crack above Herschel's head. He dodged and heard Chawa sob, "No—no, no!"

"We'll leave your things here," Abraham cried disgustedly. "Don't follow us."

One of the last things Herschel heard as he reached

the front door was Chawa's sobbing his name. "Six Rue des Petites Ecuries," she cried, "is where we'll be."

"Don't you dare come," Abraham screamed.

Often, he'd dawdle on his way to Ernst's, pausing on bridges to watch fallen leaves drift downstream; in his imagination he'd put himself in one of them and imagine how it would feel, Cleopatra in a barge, carried along gently.

But now he pushed people aside; he clawed through crowds as if half-buried, still alive under the dirt, trying to reach the surface. He ran past Madame LaRoche without stopping to ask of her lumbago, flying up the stairway, having difficulty with the key.

"Ernst," he cried out. But the apartment was empty.

The key turning in the lock shocked him. For an hour he had paced, crying out, bending over as he felt a burn of acid churning in his stomach. He tried to calm himself, as Ernst came in.

"Watch out—my briefcase!" Ernst closed the door. "What is it?"

"I have to leave."

"Why?" He held Herschel back to look him over. "So early? Did you break something?"

"No."

"What is it?"

"Remember when you asked about my past?"

"Of course."

"And I wouldn't say anything?"

He nodded, reaching for a chair.

"I don't have papers; I did not enter France legally." He held out his passport. "I have to leave."

"No. Why? Let me see!"

Herschel flung the booklet.

Still trying to smile, Ernst kneeled; he lifted the document and hurriedly glanced through it. Watching Ernst's worried face made Herschel want to scream. Ernst's eyes grew paler. He swallowed.

"What will I do? I can't stay in France; I can't return to Germany!"

"But it says your citizenship is Polish." Ernst closed the passport and held it in both his hands. "Herschel," he began, "how long have you—"

The boy turned away, did not speak.

"Well?"

Don't act like Uncle Abraham—please.

"I tried to ask for help, but you—"

"But I what?"

Herschel lowered his eyes. "Because I was Jewish, I thought maybe you'd . . . you'd think . . ." He turned away.

"That has nothing to do with anything!"

"I didn't want you to think that's what I saw in you."

Ernst's face went cold.

"I didn't want you to doubt . . ." Herschel's words ran out. "I wasn't going to ask . . ." he whispered. "And

I didn't! Ernst," he cried as flung himself forward. "I wanted to make you happy!"

He fell at Ernst's feet, slumped down on his knees.

Ernst stood above him and did not move, did not speak.

Then he did. He picked up his briefcase and went to the bedroom. He took off his tie and jacket. Herschel stayed on the floor. From the kitchen Herschel heard rattling and the icebox latch unclasp. Then a metal pot.

The hiss and splash of water from the kitchen spigot.

The kitchen was yellow, with a frosted window so no one could see across the narrow well. Ernst was slicing an onion on a board on a table against the wall when Herschel came in. There was a green bottle with red wine in it. "Are you staying?"

Herschel moved forward. "I have to! I've been thrown out."

Ernst put butter in a pan.

Herschel hovered, getting salt for the eggs even before Ernst asked for it. He kept waiting for Ernst's eyes to catch his—catch and ignite with joy and love and understanding. But he didn't look his way. And all during the meal, Ernst took precise bites of the omelet and noisily scraped the burned toast that Herschel had prepared.

Herschel did not eat.

Ernst cleared and did the dishes in the shallow sink.

"You take the bed," Ernst croaked out after the dishes were stacked. "I'll sleep out here."

Herschel was going to wipe them dry. "But. Don't you want . . . ?"

"No!" Ernst turned away. "I need to think."

The night was endless, with anxious dreams and frantic imaginings. Herschel jumped at every noise and did not stay asleep. Even before the dark windows paled, Ernst had dressed and tapped on the door. "Give me your papers—those that you have." He went toward the front door and called back, "And, if you go, don't let Madame LaRoche see you leave. We can't have her know you spent the night here."

"Ernst, please—"

The door slammed. And in a rush of nausea, Herschel ran to the water closet and crouched on the floor, his stomach heaving, but he had eaten nothing.

"I think I have a fever," he said and started to weep.

Ernst could tell that something had changed. Although early, he knew the ambassador was already in because the flag was flying. Usually, the ambassador did not arrive at work till midmorning. The air nearly vibrated with emergency; the teletype machines chimed in, with typewriters clanging. Voices went silent when doors opened and boys with messages ran in.

They tell me nothing, he wanted to complain. It seemed part of a larger conspiracy that he be ignored, looked over, not seen.

All morning Ernst sat useless in his office, staring into the rain of bright yellow leaves falling from the trees. He remembered the farm boy he had met on his bicycle trip, saw the rutted road, the tall trees. It had not been that bad, had it, being alone at night, looking at sights, speaking with Mademoiselle Taulin in the evening? A nostalgia, like remembering health when you're ill, washed over him.

Jorns was the one to talk to. If only it had not been he who had given Ernst the lecture about the Hebrew virus, the germ in the body of Germany. And, no doubt, with all this flurry of couriers and meetings and telephone calls, Jorns would be busy.

But his door was open.

Ernst stood on the threshold for a full minute; Jorns, he knew, could see him.

Ernst cleared his throat.

"Yes?" Jorns looked up. He was a brute of a man, with a dark glowering face and full fleshy lips that muscles could not control; his lips fell open and hung, pendulous, petulant. If you noticed them, Jorns would pinch them back angrily.

"Is it convenient now, sir, to ask you something?"

The undersecretary looked at the papers on his desk.

"It should just take a minute. Please."

Jorns sighed, closed the folder, locked his big hands together, and turned his somber metal-colored eyes on Ernst. "Please." He spoke sarcastically and did not ask Ernst to sit.

Ernst stepped in, tried a smile, but then abandoned

the effort. He stammered and then, staring at a spot on the window frame just above Jorns's face, he began. He told it well, he thought. Although he was sweating. But maybe Jorns would just attribute it to the change in the weather. The rain had stopped, and it was warm that morning.

When he finished, he smiled and looked Jorns in the face.

He had been filling his pipe when Ernst began, but he had frozen, his hand motionless.

"Why in the name of God would you want to help such a creature?" he asked quietly, hands again reaching for the humidor. He narrowed his eyes. "You've not gotten involved with some prostitute—you're not being blackmailed, are you?"

"No, sir!"

Jorns seemed to enjoy Ernst's blushing unease and that Jorns, a plebian, could have a vom Rath scared of him. He grunted, filling his pipe, tamping the tobacco down, shifting in his seat. "I had a friend who kept a Jewish one. A nice apartment, a maid, everything. She was a beauty but bad news."

Ernst watched him draw on his pipe, the flare of the match pulling downward to the fragrant strands. When they lit, they looked like burning worms. Smoke rose. Jorns removed the pipe from his mouth and smiled wetly. "Why this sudden interest?"

"It's a friend, a neighbor," Ernst swallowed. "Of my family. A neighbor of my family."

"Jews?" Jorns's tongue darted into the corner of his full lips.

Ernst nodded, looking away. "They're very good people, sir."

"Yes, yes. Everyone has his own special Jew. If yours is so exemplary, though, why does he need a favor for his papers?"

"It's complicated."

"Obviously. German, is he?"

"No, sir. Polish citizen, I think, living for years in Germany."

"Well!" Jorns smiled quickly. "That settles it. Last week, perhaps, but now . . ." He waved his hand. "You might have noticed how busy we are."

Ernst nodded, embarrassed.

Jorns picked up a telegram. "From Berlin early this morning—the latest. Poland, we hear, is going to refuse to renew the passports of its Jew citizens living out of the country. There's ten thousand of them in Germany."

"And?"

"The Poles are not stupid. Even they don't want Jews. When Poland refuses to let their Jews back in, they'll be stateless, and we don't want to be stuck with them." Jorns warmed to his topic. "That's why we are planning to send all Polish Jews now in Germany back across the border before the new edict goes through. So tell your 'friend,'" he mouthed the word unpleasantly, "that he is not welcome. You'll be doing him a favor to tell him to book a train seat back to Poland. Before his papers expire there too. We're not going to send ours back so comfortably."

"Oh." Ernst stood, waiting for more words, but Jorns put his pipe in its rack and opened the folder in front of him. "Now, if you don't mind."

"Thank you, sir."

"And please close the door behind you."

After he shut it, Ernst heard laughing. Right at that very moment, he knew, Jorns was scribbling, making marks in his file, blows against his personal destiny.

For a long while he did not move, just watched through the hall window as the yellow leaves fell, like pieces of the sky. Then he left. Nagorka was puzzled; for he had never seen the third secretary leave work so early.

By then Herschel's fever had peaked. Ernst closed the front door and he woke. In the bedroom the boy raised his face from the bed, a wild look in his eye. It was dark in the room. Ernst, when he came in, could barely see him.

"Is it all right?"

Ernst shook his head. "Come with me."

Herschel shivered and followed him to the chair by the window.

Ernst raised the blind. "Are you all right?"

"I don't feel well."

Ernst pursed his lips. "It'll do no good to get sick."

Herschel winced.

"You have to leave France, right?"

Herschel nodded.

"And you can't go back to Germany."

"No."

"So you know what's left?"

"I'm too small for Palestine."

Ernst jerked. "You still have your original Polish papers, don't you?"

Ernst's look made him answer directly.

"Yes."

"You'll have to leave immediately," said Ernst, who had turned away and was pacing, every now and then turning back. "No one wanted to tell me—I had to trick them into divulging—but there's a new policy to be announced. I don't know exactly when. But if you leave in a day or two, you should make it. No, don't interrupt! All Polish Jews, even with papers, who have not lived there for years, like you, Herschel, are going to lose their citizenship through decree. All in Germany will be expelled, before Poland refuses to take them back."

"But—"

"You have to get to Poland before it stops taking back its Jews," he explained. "Don't you see?"

"But . . . what?" Herschel looked around the room, dazed.

"It's probably good you don't have any family there," Ernst was saying. And that made him want to scream.

"But what about—?" Herschel blurted out.

"Us?"

Herschel nodded, swallowing.

"I don't know, Herschel. Things are moving so fast. My father will think I'm mad, and Jorns has probably already reported me, but . . ." he paced silently for a moment or two. "I'll ask for a transfer. And I'll come join you. In Warsaw. My mother visited once. She said it's lovely."

Lovely! Herschel remembered the stories, pogroms, priests in processions grabbing at you in the street to make you kiss the statue of Jesus, telling you, "Your Lord! Kiss it!"

"I want to stay, Ernst—let me, please."

"Herschel, you can't. You have to leave!"

But he did not hear; he could not stop thinking of what would happen in Poland.

"If your aunt and uncle won't help you, then I will."

Uncle Abraham. Aunt Chawa. His chest constricted. He put his hand over his mouth, as if to retch. They'd see what he was, what he had been doing.

"Herschel!"

He felt his stomach heave. "No," he shouted.

Ernst reached for him as he ran out the door.

Outside in the light, holding on to a fence, he bent over and threw up. Ernst ran down the stairs but then crept back up. Madame LaRoche was watching.

Herschel tried to think but could not focus. He felt dizzy. It seemed like weeks since he had been outside.

But he had come to Ernst's flat last night and had stayed all day in bed, sleeping, dreaming.

"I've never known anyone so lazy," Abraham sometimes would say, contempt in his eyes, as he watched Herschel on his cot in the morning.

On the curb Herschel put his hands over his ears.

"Don't you want to be of use to your family?"

And when he went to the kitchen, Chawa would ask what he had heard from home. Berta, Solly.

He could have helped them more, sent more money, but he had thought only of himself, not their suffering. He tried to keep his mind blank as he waited for Ernst to come take him back in. Herschel looked up. But it was someone else.

Together, they'd solve it. They'd hold each other in the velvet heat. At the window sun would tinge the atmosphere and burn their skin as the whole sky ignited in a pink and golden sheen. But now it was cool, night was falling, and all he could think about was Berta, pulling the Passover glasses from the straw. Her finger circled the rim, making it sing.

"You should be happy."

He had been.

After a while, there was a stir; he could feel it, like before a storm, the cool harsh air descending. A woman ran by with a ripped dress, red face, mouth curved down, eyes streaming. As he entered his neighborhood, newsboys jumped off trucks, calling out special editions.

"Polish Jews stateless," they screamed.

"What is it? What do you mean?" people cried out to those who had papers, who were reading.

Poland had invalidated the passports of its Jews living outside its borders. "We are not going to be left with them," an official at the German embassy explained. "We're rounding them up and giving them free transportation back to their country of origin. We will not be stuck with Poland's dregs—they have to leave our country."

The newspaper ran a picture of a man with dark hair and big loose lips. He was smiling.

Herschel dropped the sheet and then retrieved it.

"Herschel!" a voice called.

And he turned.

Dothan, with his friendly spaniel eyes and pitted dark skin, got up from the stoop in front of Aunt Chawa and Uncle Abraham's apartment building. Smiling, Dothan came forward with his hand extended.

"Is that any way to treat an old friend? Who's come to make you money?"

Herschel blinked and held up his hand.

"It's your old client." Dothan smiled as if he were granting a wish. "He's called. For you. This evening!"

He remembered how it had been. Blackness—but later he remembered it as red, like light seen behind closed eyes—came over him. And he was someone, something else, a beast.

"The same place," Dothan said.

When Herschel last saw him, the officer was in slacks and a white undershirt that was stretched across his chest. He stood in front of a steamed oval bathroom mirror, lathered and shaving. Herschel crept out to dress. And realized that the man was watching him from a cleared-away spot in the mirror.

"That's enough for now," he had said. "The money's by the bed. Come back when I call for you."

Herschel nodded. Exuding the smell of soap and leather, the man came over to Herschel and worked the lock, then held the door open. Herschel slid around him, looking up.

"Hey," Dothan called. "Where are you going?"

"Aunt Chawa!" Herschel screamed, running up the steps to the door, flinging it open.

But it was empty. He had forgotten. They had moved. Yesterday. Six Rue des Petite Ecuries.

That's where they must be. In the Maison Albert hollowness taunted him, with straw in corners, a pile of clothes. Wrapped in paper, spots showing through—some fruit, a cake, and cheese. The rooms echoed as he tore around them. He fell to his knees to eat. The bread was hard. He chewed for a while, then stopped, sobbing. He remembered her calling out.

What had she said?

And how Uncle Abraham had stopped her from telling. He tried to eat but could not swallow.

Herschel had a dream. He was in the center of a great big wheel that was turning. All around him, faces pirouetted like pinwheels. Solly; Ernst; strange wolf-like people, half animal, half beast, leered at him, and people laughed in a carnival scene. All were queuing up to see Herschel. A man came up—the man from the newspaper; he undressed and bent Herschel over, showing his front and back, as if he were convincing the audience that magic was about to be done here.

"My whip, please."

Herschel woke up. It was blazing hot. He felt a burning, like a flame, all over him, memory of the dream. He touched his face and wrists.

He was out walking, or was he? He stumbled by a cafe where streets met at the sides of a wedge-shaped building. The Hotel Istanbul stood across the street, the moonlight warping it. He looked up to the window, looking for himself, his ghost, his history. Like light from dead stars, it was still happening. From an angle Herschel thought he saw himself.

But it was Solly, dressed as a priest.

"Forgive me," he pleaded, but Solly took out a knife

and started carving out chunks of his flesh, offering it to children to eat. Herschel woke, sweating, coming to understand that he was sick and it was a dream.

He slept and woke periodically—to dark still nights, humid afternoons, and bustling mornings. The Maison Albert, empty, rang with echoes and dreams. People came to the door and rattled the knob; shadows played on the glass, silhouettes of fears. Time passed, days melted; it seemed like years. When the bread and fruit and cheese that Chawa had left were gone, he did not eat.

Once when he came to, he saw a mouse looking at him.

Maybe he was ill, not going mad. He went to the faucet to drink, and from out the corner of his eye, he saw something in the front hall that had been shoved under the door.

He tiptoed toward the light and saw a corner of a postcard. He recognized the handwriting.

From the files on Herschel Grynszpan (two postcards):

Herschel—
You have, of course, heard what is happening to us.

On Thursday night we heard rumors all Polish Jews would be rounded up and expelled, but everyone discounted it. At 9.00 P.M., a policeman came to our door and asked us to present our passports at the station. We took nothing, went just as we were. There, we had expulsion orders shoved into our hands. We had to leave.

We don't have anything. We haven't received your money.

—Berta

Another card was beneath it.

Dear Brother and Sister-in-law,
Our situation is hopeless. We're homeless, don't

get enough to eat. I beg you to help. We're lost. Don't forget us, please.

Sendel

Herschel put the postcards down and paced the empty rooms, the echoes making him jump. Then he found and put on the new pinstriped suit that Uncle had just made for him.

Outside, he read the newspapers that had been unfolded and pinned up on the kiosks in the Rue St. Denis. It was oddly warm, as if summer had returned, refusing to yield.

Nathan hailed him from the cafe. "Look at you—all dressed up! Where are you going?"

Herschel stopped to consider. He pulled the postcards from his coat pocket and handed them to Nathan, who read them and handed them back.

"I'm sorry, Herschel. What does it mean?"

Herschel looked at the cards with a tender smile, as if they were photographs.

"I need to be with my family."

"But that's crazy, Herschel. Look at the papers."

They were all over the tables of the cafe.

He pored over the grainy photographs of Jews pulled from their homes and shoved into trains. German border guards flinging them out into the woods, Polish guards stopping and even firing at them. Thousands camped in a no-man's land. The paper mentioned suicides, people driven crazy, thousands ill in the rain and muddy fields.

He looked for a glimpse of Berta, his parents, Solly.

He put the postcards back in his pocket and left.

He thought of Ernst, but it was Dothan he needed to see. He had to get money.

Was he speaking out loud? The way people looked at him made him wonder. One woman pulled her daughter away, and they stared from a doorway.

Things felt odd and the city broke in fragments. Hours later, he came to a familiar widening where there was a cafe with lights in the trees. He looked up and saw a window in the Hotel Istanbul. And in the cafe below, people were drinking, laughing.

He heard music from a grizzled organ grinder. His monkey, wearing a crusty red vest, took off its hat and asked for money. The monkey had curved yellow teeth and made copulating movements; girls shrieked, jumping into the arms of their boyfriends. The organ grinder caught the eye of one happy fellow and winked.

From an angle, a tangle in the crowd, Herschel thought he saw someone he knew.

Their eyes met and the look on Ernst's face skyrocketed from recognition to excitement and relief. Herschel averted his gaze, as if from something embarrassing.

"Where have you been? Herschel!" Ernst seemed both relieved and frenzied. "Herschel!" He drew him in and would have hugged him more, but the boy pulled back. "What's happening? Why didn't you come to me all these nights? I've been looking for you! I knocked and knocked. Your uncle's apartment is empty!"

"My aunt and uncle moved," he said dully, trying to deny the happiness, the relief, trying to come up with an explanation for how the world could have changed so quickly.

"What have you been doing?" Ernst asked.

"Nothing. I was sick. I have to leave."

"I know," Ernst agreed. "I've been keeping my ears open at the embassy. I kept trying to find you."

He reached out to stroke Herschel's hand, but the boy jerked away. He needed suffering.

Ernst's eyes grew large. "I'm sorry! I'm sorry. What did I do? Sit with me. For a minute. Please." Ernst steered him to a cafe with tables under canvas awnings and trees. Every time the waiter came, they fell silent. Herschel watched his glass, with its broken reflections of light and night spiraling together dizzyingly.

"Herschel." He looked at the glass's patterns. "What are you thinking?"

His lips twitched; his face burned.

"It doesn't matter."

"Why?"

"It's too late. You can't do anything for me."

Ernst swallowed. "Was that all I was to you?"

Ernst looked so hurt. Herschel shook his head, tenderly mouthed, "no."

Ernst reached across the table and squeezed his fingers. "I've ached for this, Herschel." Slowly tears appeared. "I've missed you. I thought I'd never have a chance. But as soon as I saw you, I knew." He wiped his eyes and smiled. "You changed me. Remember those nights in our room?"

It hurt Herschel to see a face that was not his own so full of suffering. He glanced at the glass in Ernst's hands.

"I never wanted this," Ernst said, looking in its depths, as if their pasts, their lives, were mixed in that tangle of broken light and bent deformed images. "You know that, don't you?"

"Wanted what?"

"The diplomatic corps, the embassy. But my family made me." He looked away. "Do you understand?"

Herschel shook his head, knowing he was lying. His family had been pushed back to Poland; they, not he, were suffering. And now they were making him do something. "I love them! Ernst, I lied to you," Herschel said. "They're alive—my parents. I have a brother, a sister."

"What do you mean?"

"It was wrong! I wanted to be free. But—"

The boy jumped up, made violently to leave, but Ernst stopped him with a whisper.

"It's all right, Herschel. You can't save them. Come away with me."

Herschel froze. A thrill, a chill, ran up his spine.

"We'll forget everything—just you and me. We'll go south. To the Mediterranean, a house by the sea."

Herschel pictured white walls, arched windows, a blue ocean, and fringed trees. Ernst and he on white sand and sheets.

"I can't! I've got postcards, they need help, they need—"

"Here," Ernst stood and handed over big bills. "Send it to them. Herschel. Take it for them, but come with me. We'll escape. We'll live just for us, ourselves, only."

Herschel reached for the money just as a gendarme's whistle blew. He leapt up, tipping the table; the glass smashed and all the images fractured too.

"Come back," Ernst cried as Herschel fled.

"The French police are after me."

After midnight he stopped and sat; he tried to think clearly—and saw only two things to do: Be miserable. Save his family. He cringed till he noticed a nearby window with a light blinking on and off. The light winked through the diamond-shaped wire mesh; the glass was thick, green almost, eerie.

He came up and pressed closer, resting his head on the cool glass window. The objects in there, the locks and guns, seemed to want to tell him something.

After a long while he turned away. He rented a room in the Hotel Istanbul for one night only.

Alone this time, the clerk thought. But then he shrugged, knowing that such things could not last with degenerates such as he.

I knew then what I had to do. I'd go back in the morning. And then take it to the embassy. That would make them listen to me.

But I was sick. I did not sleep. But with my family in need, that's all that mattered. It was all so clear and easy. I knew. It did not matter what happened to me.

Madame Carpe, small and gentle, smiled that next morning as she raised the shop window's awning with a metal crank. It seemed like she was creating the sun, pulling forth the light, with her key.

"I want to buy a gun." The words sounded beautiful, like poetry.

"That's my husband's job," she explained, nodding at the figure within.

"He was very calm," the precise little man with a dainty mustache later told the police. (He had come forward after recognizing the picture of the boy in the paper that morning.) "He said he worked for an uncle and often had to carry large sums of money. He showed me some."

He had opened the glass case and taken out a small nickel pistol with a tortoiseshell handle; it lay on a velvet board, like jewelry.

"I showed him how to load it, aim, and shoot. He gave me cash. I tied the packages up, the revolver in one brown paper parcel, the bullets in another. With string." (The police would find the paper and string in a bathroom at the Café Tout Va Bien.)

"I told him he had to register it with the police, and he went out, saying he would. But he went the wrong way up the street."

A half-hour later Herschel emerged from the Metro on the Boulevard St. Germain and stopped to get his bearings.

I don't know how I got there. I went for my people. I was going to make them proud of me.

Herschel felt slow, in a dream, as if his feet hovered, did not hit the street.

He seemed to hear cheering as he was drawn to the black swastika on a banner of red, floating over the embassy.

"I have secrets," he confessed. "I am not me." A moment before, he had wanted to turn back, but now with the gate opening, and the ringing of bells, he felt the beckoning of destiny.

"The ambassador is not in," he was told. And his assistant, Jorns, was not seeing anybody. Would he settle for—

"Yes!" he said without hearing.

"His eyes were strange," Nagorka said. "But I did what I was told. I took him to the officer on duty."

I made my plan as I entered; as I walked up the hall, it became clear. What I had bought the gun for, why I was at the embassy.

I would make my demands to the ambassador to rescue

my family. I would pull the gun and make him telephone from his office. And if he refused, then I would kill myself in front of him. So the world would know, and see what was happening to Jews in Germany.

Everyone would see Herschel Grynszpan was not afraid; everyone could see how I was willing to suffer for my family.

How surprised they'd be back home. And Uncle Abraham would feel horrible, guilty.

"Knock and go in," the porter told him.

He knocked and opened the door.

He thought he was dreaming as the door closed and Ernst jumped up from his chair. "Herschel, thank God! Why did you run away?"

Herschel smiled. He just stood there blinking.

"Herschel, what is it? What's wrong? Are you ready? Right now. Let's leave."

"No," he said. "You're not the ambassador."

"Why do you want to see him? Herschel, what you said at the gate about secrets, what did you mean?"

"My family and people have been mistreated," he recalled. "I need to make a statement."

"But it was not me, Herschel. What have you got there? What are you doing? We can flee, Herschel— just you and I together—"

"No!"

"We can help your family!"

"Don't speak of them," he blubbered, as he fell to his knees.

Ernst ran over. "Herschel." He pressed him to his chest.

"The time together, what we did . . ." Herschel faltered. The joy, the pleasure. "It was wrong."

"No! What we had, what we have—"

"It was selfish, it was ugly!" Herschel was in tears.

"You don't believe that!"

"I do! I hated it!" he cried in agony. Ernst needed to be punished too. "I'll tell the ambassador . . ."

Ernst fell back. "Is that the secret you have?"

His face was pale. "Are you going to tell about . . . us . . . me?"

And then he saw the gun.

I was going to shoot myself. The ambassador wasn't in. No one would help me.

Herschel wept and put the barrel of the gun into his mouth.

"Don't!"

"I have to!" He had to take it out to speak.

He was putting it back in, closing his eyes, fingers tensing. He felt cruel. "I never loved you."

"No—that's not true!"

Ernst leaped forward to kiss him. Herschel jerked and dropped the gun. It danced, a demon. Bullets ricocheted; holes opened in walls; plaster rained from the ceiling.

Ernst was calling his name and then looked puzzled

as he lurched crazily. He walked like a drunken man, Charlie Chaplin; his head flopped to one side.

"No!" Herschel shouted, jumping for the gun. "Not you! Me!"

The door burst open. Nagorka stopped at what he saw.

"Help him," Herschel screamed.

As they led him down, dazed and not speaking, into the street, he looked back. He heard an ambulance approaching.

"Jew! Murderer!" someone on the street screamed.

Flashbulbs popped. Herschel raised his arm in front of his face.

That was the picture that appeared in papers all over the world the next morning.

Szwarc had put the newspaper down, but took it up again to look at the photograph of Herschel. It was appealing, more than the boy.

He took a turn around the room, assessing Herschel from all angles, his thick lashes, dark child's face pouting with sullen prettiness. An idea hit him.

He went to the cell door, motioning to Vessine-Larue.

"Where can I find a telephone?" he asked the first person he ran into. The guard pointed down a streamlined hallway.

Vessine-Larue followed, cocking his head. "What is it?"

Szwarc was already speaking from the booth and waved him away: "You're sure then? The same day?! All right. No, I won't. Nobody." He put the receiver down. Szwarc stared at the phone, as if he wanted to argue with it. Vessine-Larue raised his eyebrows instead of asking what was happening.

"It's no good." Szwarc blew out a sigh, getting up from the built-in seat. "He knows Grynszpan!"

"Who?"

"The pimp you got off last year—the boy one. Dothan! He got a call a few days ago—from 'someone important' is all he would say—for Herschel's services; someone who sounded German!"

Vessine-Larue went pale; it made his hair seem more orange. "Do you think?"

Szwarc nodded.

"What does it mean?"

"For us? A rent boy shooting his mark is not world news. We'll be the laughingstock of Paris if the story gets out." He turned away. And then back. "We won't, we can't, tell anybody."

Vessine-Larue nodded. "But what if he talks?"

"The boy? Not likely."

"But vom Rath—if he recovers?"

Szwarc paused. "It would be stupid for him to admit it." He pointed at the telephone. "Call the clinic. See how's he's doing."

Ernst heard someone say his name. Surely, it was a dream, for suddenly his mother, tall and thin, gray hair loose and eyes shinning, was staring down at him. She held the back of her cool hand to his hot forehead.

He blinked. As he grew up, she had never shown affection—father called it "coddling." But he liked it. He opened his eyes again. The room cleared, and he saw his two handsome brothers standing wide-eyed behind her. Blond Guenther waved unsurely and darker Gustav reached out and brushed his brother's cheek. Ernst wrinkled his forehead, opened his mouth. But his mother put a finger to his lips.

"We took the fast train in," she explained, stroking his hand. Then she linked her fingers in his, bringing her face down. "My son."

His tall father leaned in.

"You've been promoted!"

Ernst labored, tried to sit up, to come to attention, but his father put his hand on his shoulder and pushed him down. "Save your breath. You're a hero, son."

He lay back, perplexed, but then smiled. "Herschel," he tried but coughed. "How is he?" "The ambassador's fine," his father beamed. "And you've earned special thanks—see?" He withdrew to let the doctors approach.

"Who?"

"Adolf Hitler," Dr. Magnus said, bending so close that Ernst could smell his sour breath, "sent us to take care of you." He bent closer. "Tell me how you are feeling."

"He did not mean it. It was an accident," Ernst whispered.

Brandt nodded. "Of course. We understand. Don't worry." He swabbed Ernst's arm and held a syringe. It stung. "No talking. Sleep. Make your Führer happy." Ernst had a strange idea.

"See," Magnus said in satisfaction, turning to the vom Raths. "Resting better already. Reich drugs are better than what the French can muster."

In the late afternoon, mellow light streamed through the blinds, and the room swam in warmth; Ernst's mother bent down. "My boy," she whispered in his ear, as she used to, stealing into the nursery at night to assure him that she was near. I should have done this more often, she thought; from now on she'd follow her own thinking. "Ernst," she whispered. "Talk to me."

He gurgled, his eyes fluttered.

"Ernst," his father prompted, "your mother is speaking."

His hand dropped from hers and she screamed.

Gustav and Guenther, startled awake, jumped from their seats.

Dr. Magnus appeared.

"No!" Herschel shrieked. He pulled away from Szwarc, who was trying to hold him, make him listen. "You're wrong. It can't be! Your partner said he would get better." He started to cry, grow wild. "It's a lie. You're lying."

"I just heard from the hospital," Szwarc said. He shook the boy. "Now, listen. You'll be charged with murder. You need me."

"But I didn't mean it. It was an accident! He saved me!"

Szwarc looked around. "Be quiet, people will hear."

"Ernst!"

"You don't know what you're saying."

"I do, I do!" Herschel pulled free; he started to shudder and weep. "Ernst, I did!" He ran around the room. "I loved you!"

"STOP!" Szwarc took a giant step forward and was ready to slap his cheek. "Look!" he held up the diary.

"This is the truth. You say right here, vom Rath struck you, shouted 'Jew.' This is what happened, you hear? You did it for your family." He struck the page. "You have to say these things."

In Munich the minister of the thousand-year Reich smiled at the news. With everything now under control, he could enjoy the pageantry. How genuine and spontaneous it would seem, even though he knew that it had been planned, down to the last slamming car door and cooing blond baby. It was like the fairy tales he told his golden-haired children when Magda brought them in before sleep. Even as he made things up, he believed what he was saying. That was the magic of myth and the man to save Germany.

He entered the crowd just as the Führer's automobile appeared. As the black car door opened and the great man emerged, the crowd broke into pandemonium. Mothers held up babies; grandmothers wept; blond-haired girls in native costumes curtsied.

The great man walked forward, solemnly carrying an enormous urn of flowers that had been placed at the curb. He mounted sixteen shallow steps to a platform decked with sixteen swastika-draped funeral biers, big black looming pylons draped with crepe. The numbers were mystical, they had meanings, and were being repeated to make indentations, impressions on the clay of destiny. He put the flowers down and stood at attention, his gloved hands behind him, looking down at the empty symbolical coffins.

The crowds strained forward to see. After a moment, Hitler turned to the multitudes and raised his hands. Something like thunder boomed from the people; all saluted at once, and one could almost feel the current run from Hitler's hand to theirs as they reached out. It was Armageddon, the ground cracking, obeisance to a power that could not be ignored, a destiny that they now decreed.

Smiling in his secret space of joy and mystic wonder, the propaganda minister watched the Führer pull devotion from the crowd; he could feel it, like magnetism or heat. Goebbels's heart nearly burst with pride, his long dark face streaked with tears. The journey had been long—today was the fifteenth anniversary of the day that sixteen party members had died in a beer hall revolt to take the country. (Next year, imagine the convergence of numbers—sixteen and sixteen!) Their souls had come back, he could feel them, as everyone grew anxious for the apotheosis that awaited. Just as the crowd looked up, wondering where the sound came from, they appeared—sixteen airplanes passing overhead in the pattern of a swastika. The minister exulted. "We own the skies! We rule the seas!"

As the names of the sixteen dead were read and flames leaped from sixteen pyres behind the biers, sixteen times the crowd cried "Here."

What a gift from the gods, this action of the Jew Grynszpan's was, on the eve of the Nazi Party's anniversary.

That night thousands sat at tables, red flags hanging from the rafters of the hall, eagles and swastikas adorning the building that, like the new Germany, was modern and sleek and fierce. On the podium sat dignitaries, speaking to each other, looking out over the torchlit audience. The Führer sat aloof, as if summoning power for his speech. Only he was unaware of the young handsome blond man in a black cap who parted the crowd in the hall and slowly approached the head table. The boy trembled, extending a telegram.

The great man stirred, saw the boy, smiled benignly.

The young man saluted and handed it over.

Everyone grew silent as if to overhear. The great leader put down his napkin, slowly and delicately unfolding the yellow telegram. As he read it, his face showed nothing. He crushed the piece of paper in his fist.

Goebbels looked stricken; he nodded and snapped to attention, as everyone at the head table did, some leaping to their feet as the great man turned smartly to the right and left the platform.

The propaganda minister stooped to retrieve the yellow sheet that Hitler had dropped. Slowly, he flattened it, passing his hand over it again and again, showing it to some of the men on the podium. The entire hall was at a standstill by the time the minister moved to the microphone. When he tapped it, the sound exploded, startling everyone.

"This is tragic and grave news just in! It concerns the one for whom we have been praying, whom we hold most dear." His voice rose.

"Ernst vom Rath was a brave German, toiling for all of us, all of us here. In Paris, while at work, he, with no weapons, suspecting nothing, went to confer with a visitor who had cold-bloodedly asked for him. He was shot twice and is now dead."

The thousands stopped milling. Goebbels let go of the paper and watched it flutter to the floor.

"Do I need to tell you the race of the creature that executed this deed?"

"Jew!"

"Yes! Tonight the coward is in a jail in Paris but tells lies, saying he acted on his own and was not part of a world conspiracy. But we are wise; and know better, don't we?"

"Yes!" the crowd cheered.

"His act must be answered." He struck his fist on the podium and the microphone sang. "Our people must know what has happened, they must be told, and they must repudiate the Jew."

Cruel smiles. Echoing cheers.

"We must act!"

"Act! Act!" the crowds echoed; some people ran out of the building.

"To the Jews."

Shouts in the street.

"What now?" Herschel asked, seeing the slack, pale, grieving faces of his attorneys. Szwarc looked like he had not slept in days, and Vessine-Larue was so white he seemed about to faint.

"What's happening?"

Entering, they brought in a chill from a changed world. They put four newspapers down on the table and then turned, without saying a word. Herschel approached the table, the papers, cautiously, as if they could hurt him.

He looked. He blinked.

NIGHT OF POGROMS, he read. RETALIATIONS FOR MURDER OF DIPLOMAT VOM RATH IN PARIS EMBASSY.

Reich Kristallnacht; night of broken glass; in Germany.

"Spontaneous" demonstrations had erupted all over once the news of vom Rath's death was released.

In nearly every major city mobs had turned on Jews, killing, burning, destroying neighborhoods, throwing people and possessions out of windows to the street.

They looted and ransacked Jewish businesses. They smashed nearly every window of every Jewish-owned shop in Germany.

The Nazis burned down synagogues, rounded up Jews, and marched them past taunting crowds. Photographs showed old men, beards shorn, beaten, forced to clean streets with toothbrushes dipped in acid. People screamed and laughed with glee, held up babies to see Jews being tortured and young women, arms in front of their naked breasts, running down streets. Several thousand Jewish men were rounded up and marched to concentration camps.

Guards pointed guns, while citizens hurled garbage and spit and hit Jews on the head with pig feces.

NEW POLICIES FOR JEWS IN EFFECT IN GERMANY.

There were shells of burned-out synagogues, Stars of David on walls, "Death to Jew Grynszpan" scrawled on the sides of buildings.

Scores were dead, others in jail, more injured and in hiding.

JEWS TO PAY FOR THE DAMAGES.

A Jew had struck at the heart of the Fatherland. So the folk had fought back. It was all spontaneous, decreed Joseph Goebbels, the minister of propaganda. The police had tried to intervene, but the German people were uncontrollable, understandable given the nature of the vile assassin's act.

DEATH TO INTERNATIONAL JEWRY.

All German officials interviewed said that Germany would have a new Jewish policy now. Jews had to be dealt with severely.

For days afterward Herschel, nauseated with grief, could not eat or speak. He sat on his bed, head in hands, dizzy with the swimming responsibility and unreality. Guilt, like paralysis or the darkness from a vast bottomless pit, seeped into his cell. It came in a whisper and he knew. It was true. But all he had wanted . . .

Several days passed before he allowed his attorneys back in. Vessine-Larue rushed forward in a tumble and fell to his knees.

"No—" Herschel turned away. He would not accept help. The time had come, at last, for his overdue suffering.

"Help us, please."

"Move!" the boy cried, shoving him. He was going to die here.

Szwarc came forward, hands out.

"Herschel, listen." Herschel tried to put his hands over his ears, but Szwarc pried them off, the boy still struggling. Herschel closed his eyes and cried out in pain, so he would not hear. Szwarc noted the ravages of the past days.

"It's over now, Herschel. Finished."

Herschel shook his head, but Szwarc insisted, "All over the world, people are rallying, journalists are speaking out. Committees have come together to mount a defense for you."

Herschel turned away.

"It's true!"

The most famous radio journalist in America, Dorothy Thompson, had spoken to the English-speaking world about a strange Polish Jew named Herschel Grynszpan.

"Last Thursday," she said on the radio.

"Last Thursday," she said, her words echoing all over the world, *"an anemic-looking boy with brooding black eyes walked quietly into the German embassy . . . and asked to see the ambassador. He was shown into the office of the third secretary . . . and shot him.*

"Back in Germany, in every city an organized and methodical mob was turned loose on the Jewish population. . . .

In cold blood, the German government imposed a fine of four hundred million dollars on the entire Jewish community, and followed it by decrees which mean total ruin for all of them. . . . In the United states, nearly every newspaper protested.

"But in Paris, a boy who had hoped to make some gesture of protest which would call attention to the wrongs done his race burst into hysterical sobs. . . . Half a million of his fellows had been sentenced to extinction on the excuse of his deed.

"I am speaking of this boy."

Herschel was entranced. How could she know such things?

"Soon he will go on trial. . . . But is there not a higher justice in the case of Herschel Grynszpan, seventeen years old? Is there not a higher justice that says that this deed has been expatiated with four hundred million dollars and half a million existences, with beatings, and burnings, and deaths and suicides?

"Who is on trial in this case? I say we are all on trial. . . . The Nazi government has announced that if any Jews, anywhere in the world, protest at anything that is happening, further oppressive measures will be taken. They are holding every Jew in Germany as a hostage.

"Therefore, we who are not Jews must . . . speak our sorrow and indignation and disgust in so many voices that they will be heard. This boy has become a symbol, and the responsibility for his deed must be shared by those who caused it."

"Son," Szwarc whispered lovingly. "The worst is over. Help is coming. This changes everything."

"What, what do you mean?" Herschel stuttered. All over the world people knew his name, his suffering. There was a roaring in his ears.

"Money's pouring in."

Vessine-Larue nodded. "But that's not why we're here, Herschel. We want to help you!"

Herschel blinked. Something like hope, a choking growth, rose in him. After all the guilt and horror, all those mistakes, the grief, now maybe . . .

Szwarc whispered in his ear. "Forty thousand dollars so far." The whisper was urgent and warm: "We can get rid of him." He motioned to the pale Vessine-Larue. "But I know your secret!"

He swung around. Szwarc smiled; Herschel was going to speak but stopped when he heard a key inserted in the lock and the knock on the door that signaled that a guard was letting someone in.

It was Uncle Solomon! Herschel wanted to rush forward but stopped and averted his face, as if expecting a blow.

Solomon said nothing. After a moment Herschel peeked. He caught his uncle's eye. Solomon half-smiled and rubbed his hands together, looking away too.

"Where's Uncle Abraham? Aunt Chawa?"

"In jail."

Herschel sank a bit.

"They've been arrested for harboring you."

"My parents?"

Uncle Solomon shrugged his shoulders and looked uncomfortable, but then, like a child unable to control his excitement, he broke out: "Herschel, darling. Good news! I'm getting you, he's coming now, he's out in the hall, the committee of your defense wants him — France's greatest attorney. Have you ever heard of Vincent de Moro Giafferi?"

Solomon smiled. "The best attorney in France, Herschel! A good man, a great man! A former minister," he said rhapsodically. "I got him for you. Right now, he's coming!"

"No!" Vessine-Larue cried.

Szwarc's eyes blazed. "We'll sue!"

"You'll be paid off." Uncle Solomon looked away. "I'm his uncle. Who are you? Nobody!"

The attorneys started to argue. "You gave us your word that you would speak to no other attorney."

"Moro Giafferi lied, fabricated stories to get the boy off," Szwarc would tell his listeners in the coming years.

But when asked what he knew to be the truth, the old man would lose fire, lose intensity. Lighting one more cigarette, he'd just say, "The boy was sick. He deserved what happened to him."

Szwarc and Uncle Solomon were arguing. With all the work that they had done, all they had already achieved . . .

"Why listen to people you do not know?" Vessine-Larue pitched in. Dorothy Thompson was a foreigner across the sea. Certainly, Moro Giafferi was a great man; certainly, he had had a distinguished career. And the case against the boy, what he faced, was daunting. But still.

In the cell everything was moving swiftly.

Outside in the hall a dark short man in a thick dark coat and black homburg appeared. Uncle Solomon fidgeted, Szwarc smiled, and Vessine-Larue looked uneasy. Moro Giafferi entered the room. He nodded at Solomon, who returned the gesture quickly.

Moro Giafferi then sighed and took off his hat. He had dark rings under his somber eyes, a thick nose, cheeks bluish from a heavy beard. Beneath his salt-and-pepper mustache was his massive mouth of crowded teeth. Herschel could not take his eyes off him but cowered as the man came toward him, as if he were going to be hit.

But the kindness in the man's eyes calmed him. He took Herschel's hands, bent a bit forward, and seemed about to kiss them. Instead, he just held the boy's hands and squeezed.

"Herr Grynszpan?"

Herschel nodded.

"What you have done!," Moro Giafferi sighed, looking into Herschel's eyes, going back and forth, and up and down, like the scales of justice.

Herschel nodded and his knees buckled. Moro Giafferi grabbed him.

"I need to speak to you right away," he said, taking him by the elbow. He had to touch, mold him. He'd overwhelm Herschel and leave him no time to think.

He led the boy to two chairs set next to each other to make a settee.

Herschel, dizzy in the smell of stale tobacco smoke, sat and looked at the great man's feet.

"I want to help you, young man. Will you let me?"

Herschel looked up. "No, I need to be—"

"Please," Moro Giafferi interrupted. "No foolishness." Herschel looked down abruptly. The lawyer's keen eyes were on him. "Tell me why you did it."

Herschel opened his mouth. He tried words. "I . . . was going to shoot myself . . . to make a statement."

He looked to Szwarc, who smiled and nodded; he turned back to Moro Giafferi. "I caused all those deaths in Germany."

Moro Giafferi was impassive. "Are you scared?"

The boy nodded.

"Only one of my clients has ever gone to the guillotine."

Herschel's stomach went liquid.

"You will survive, son. You will have grandchildren."

No response.

"You will see your family."

The boy lifted his dark pitiful eyes to Szwarc; they

were liquid with tears. "I want to see them," he said. "That's why I went to the embassy."

"Yes," Szwarc cried. "I got his story down—it was difficult, but . . . "

Szwarc approached with the open diary in his hands, holding it out like an offering. Moro Giafferi waved him back, nodding as if he already knew that. He turned to Herschel.

"Do you love your family?"

"Yes! They're all I have—I never . . ." he rushed on, breathless, afraid someone would halt, contradict him, but then he faltered, as if at a cliff.

"You want to help them?"

"Yes."

"Do you hate Germans?"

He thought of Ernst.

"How about what they stand for, what they are doing to your people?"

Herschel nodded.

"I do too." Moro Giafferi said. "That's why I am here."

Herschel's heart surged with sudden hope. "All those dead—"

"Put them out of your mind; you are not to blame—Germans killed them. Not you. I know it is natural to feel guilty. Listen. Will you? I sense you don't want to."

Herschel froze.

"Help me," Moro Giafferi coaxed, "please."

Herschel hesitated.

"Promise you'll do all I ask of you."

He wavered.

"If not for you, yourself, then others: your people, your family."

Yes, that, Moro Giafferi saw, was the key.

"I'll do anything for them." The boy's look was urgent, defiant, frightened. "They're all I have left."

Moro Giafferi smiled.

"I may ask many sacrifices."

"Yes," he shouted.

"Good. That's all I need to hear." Moro Giafferi pushed his chair back and rose, with Herschel clinging to his arm. Herschel held tighter, but Moro Giafferi freed himself. He bent over and whispered in Herschel's ear: "I'll come back tomorrow at nine, and then we will speak. Alone." He gestured at Herschel's uncle and the two attorneys, who had fallen silent and were obviously trying to hear. "Without them." It was as if he were setting up a tryst. "Just you and me, son, you and me."

Herschel grabbed at his sleeve.

"I apologize for this brief visit. I just had to see you, to see if you would trust me. And I you." Then he turned. "Gentlemen?" He smiled broadly and gestured to Uncle Solomon and Szwarc and Vessine-Larue. "Will you come with me?"

They looked confused, grabbed up their coats, and agreed. To Herschel, Moro Giafferi said as he left, "I'll see you in the morning."

173

The cell door closed. Herschel stood, dazed, as if the pressure had dropped, as if he were in a new world. He suddenly had the urge to laugh and sing!

Happy, relieved, he realized he'd see Berta again! And Solly!

But that night he looked out his window and watched the moon rise and ride heedless over the city. Its light rose up like water, sliding up the side of the buildings. It inched its way up the sill. But as it spilled over and poured into his room, he withdrew. He backed away from it, would not allow it to touch him.

He'd confess in the morning, tell Moro Giafferi of Ernst, the accident, his relations with his family.

But when Moro Giafferi came, he was not alone.

"This is Henri Torres," Moro Giafferi said, indicating the other gentleman. "Herschel Grynszpan."

"I'm very honored to meet you," Torres said, bowing. He was tall and thin with a drooping moustache, attenuated, almost pulled, like taffy. Herschel didn't speak, just looked at Moro Giafferi questioningly.

"Monsieur Torres will be joining us on the defense team. He was very successful in winning the release of Samuel Schwarzbad—a Jewish lad like you who killed a Ukrainian for starting a pogrom." Moro Giafferi and Torres spoke again for a bit, then Moro Giafferi turned to Herschel. "I need to be somewhere else, to see about postponing your trial date. We have much research to do. So, tell Henri everything—in total confidence. Speak to him as if to me."

"What type of research?" Herschel called out. "Don't go," he said in a small voice. "Tell me."

Moro Giafferi looked up from his watch and smiled at Herschel.

"I've got an idea."

"A very good one," Torres put in.

"Thank you, Henri. Sit." They all did. "We will be honest with you, Herschel. This is a very charged situation. The French are terrified of you—because Germany is armed to the teeth. Judges and politicians are frightened that France will be attacked or invaded. War might be declared if you are found not guilty. Which is what will happen. I promise we will get you out of here. But we have to proceed carefully."

"And do research?" Herschel asked.

"Exactly. Germany has passed these new race laws against the Jews—the whole world is watching. So what we propose to do," he broke off and looked around, as to see if anyone could be listening. He lowered his voice. "We will gather information—on how Jews have been treated before this; we'll show the world that it was not just you and vom Rath in that room but that you were reacting to all the horrors and indignities done to your people, your family.

"Ernst vom Rath, from all we can tell, was not a rabid party member, was a kind man, we hear, and not vicious. So we need to show that it was not him you were reacting to—but to Hitler and his policies of mistreating Jews.

"It's Germany we are going to put on trial, Herschel—while the French are trying you, we are going to put Germany on trial for all the world to see."

"Oh," Herschel said.

"All Jews in German territories are now depending on you," Moro Giafferi stressed. "We wouldn't want anything to happen to them, would we?"

Herschel shook his head but could not really hear. He could not get beyond certain thoughts or scenes. Sometimes it was Solly and Berta. Other times he saw the surprise on Ernst's face, opening his mouth to speak, blood bubbling out. He started to weep.

"I'm sorry if I've burdened you," Moro Giafferi said, getting up. He chucked Herschel under the chin. "Cheer up. I'll try to find out how your family is. You've had cards from Poland? You've heard from them?"

Herschel nodded. "Tell them I love them, please."

"I will."

Moro Giafferi smiled and waved as if pronouncing a benediction.

"Now," Henri Torres said, sitting down at the table and uncapping his pen.

"Let's begin."

The next afternoon Moro Giafferi returned, saying he had gotten an extension. And he told Herschel that the Red Cross had located his family, and they were as well as could be expected. They were now out of the fields at the border, back in a small town in Poland.

"Can they come?"

Moro Giafferi shook his head. "The Polish government thinks they'll be invaded if they make Berlin angry. And Berlin does not want your family talking to the world about what just happened. Then all would know what they, and what you, have been through."

The boy stared.

"Did you hear?"

Again Herschel nodded. But Moro Giafferi added, "We have to be careful; we have to go slowly, think of everything."

Herschel sat up. He tried to pay attention to Moro Giafferi's recitation—of loopholes to close, others to go through. He saw their pale stark faces. He saw his family mired in the mud, in wooden bunks back in Poland. Moro Giafferi glanced over and broke off his monologue.

"Are you all right?"

Herschel nodded but looked green.

"You'll still help us, won't you?"

He wanted to say no, don't make me. But he nodded again.

"Excellent!" Moro Giafferi said. "I'll be back. Tomorrow."

But Moro Giafferi did not see Herschel again for weeks—just sending him word as the trial date was set and postponed repeatedly. And whenever Moro Giafferi did come, he never came alone but with someone new for the defense team.

It seemed an endless stream. Day by day, week by week, Moro Giafferi had brought each one in singly and had presented him like a gift, as if he, Herschel, were royalty. But Herschel failed to register their faces or their names. Weill-Goudchaux, he was told, had been chosen for his contacts with the World Jewish Congress.

Torres was the first one, Herschel remembered vaguely. He seemed numb and always needed to be reminded of things. The one time that the whole team had all come to his cell together, he had felt unworthy; he had wanted to give these people something—a message, a word of gratitude, an apology. He wanted to reach into his life and give them joy and youth and years, those things in which he no longer had an interest or need. So while they talked and consulted, he sat impassively.

"See?" Moro Giafferi cried, suddenly inspired to hold up Herschel's chin. He turned the boy's head back and forth. "A nice boy, not tied up in politics or anything. The jury will understand that he did not shoot vom Rath on purpose but was at wit's end. They'll set you free."

Moro Giafferi continued: "And we will show the world that all the Jews being punished in Germany are guiltless too. We'll hold Hitler and his henchmen up to world opinion. We'll save the Jews, and you."

Herschel cried out, tried to speak—he could not let them think—

"No," Moro Giafferi said, "no false modesty, please. We are all depending on you. Be strong." The attorneys smiled and nodded, and two or three came up later and shook his hand, telling Herschel how moved they were by his modesty.

For Herschel words made no sense. He stared at his hands; they had held the gun that had killed Ernst. But in his heart he had held the word whose utterance might have made it all unnecessary. The word was like a bird, and as he clutched it still, he felt its wings beat and then cease. It was dead now, and he had to let it go. Herschel stood and said it.

"I loved him."

"What did you say?" Henri Torres asked, confused.

But the boy just shook his head. He did not know to whom he was speaking as he turned to all the men in his cell and said, "Forgive me." All was ashes, grief.

He was a famous man, Moro Giafferi; he heard himself called brilliant. He hailed from Corsica, as did Napoleon, and was as short and powerful as the emperor had been. When the lawyer went home in the evenings, everyone he passed on the street bowed or nodded. He was respected for all he had done, and he was proud of his past and his current actions too, proud specifically of this defense strategy. He knew it would free Herschel Grynszpan.

He would get the boy off, but oddly (he hated to admit), he who had known statesmen, great writers, artists, and politicians, and who could deduce motivations and sense fears, was stumped by the creature with wild eyes and dark hair that stared at him.

Sometimes, just before leaving his office, he'd stop and think about Herschel Grynszpan.

The boy did not seem to be present in the room when they were speaking. Something held his eye just out of the line of vision. Something in the past held him, kept him from engaging.

Moro Giafferi never had met anyone so vague and unformed. Herschel was in a fog all the time, looking around, jumping like he was hearing things.

Perhaps he had suffered too much. Or was hiding something.

He wondered what it might be; and he thought of Herschel at odd moments during the day and at night sometimes before he fell asleep. Moro Giafferi pictured the boy as the lawyer looked at himself shaving in the mirror in the morning.

But it didn't matter what he was hiding; he was just a tool.

For as the days passed, with the memos, with money, Moro Giafferi could not worry about Herschel—only about what he could mean. He was the key to turning back all that oppression bursting forth in Germany. The boy was not important—he was only a means to an ending.

He and his men charted what was happening in Germany with clippings, notes from the press, and colleagues who reported back to them.

The decrees became wilder and wilder. Years later, when Moro Giafferi would speak of these times, he would recall how he began to worry that maybe his idea was not working.

"France understood what I was doing," he'd muse ruefully. The judges, always in the pocket of the government, saw he wanted to put Germany on trial—so if Herschel were freed, Germany would be guilty.

And angry. At France. "I knew why the boy's trial date was delayed again and again. They'd keep Herschel in jail forever, if politicians got their way."

(And they did. Herschel Grynszpan became the juvenile held longest without a trial in all of French legal history.)

So the lawyer had to do something. But what that was, what he planned to do, was too disturbing.

One night in May, Moro Giafferi called a meeting. The defense team ate quickly and then opened discussion.

He sat around the table with the other members and showed them the folders with piles of notes and clippings.

"There are tens of thousands of Jewish men in Dachau now," he recounted. "The persecution is growing. No Jews on streetcars; no Jews can have gentile employees. Jews have to give up all their belongings if they want to leave the country."

Holding Germany up to the light had not stopped the Nazis.

And around the table, sad faces agreed.

Moro Giafferi laid his head down on the smooth wooden table that gleamed like an ideal. After a few minutes he stood up again and paced, talking gravely in a low voice. Horrified, the team leaned in, listening. (In the future he'd never speak of this evening.)

Moro Giafferi watched their faces change from disappointment to disdain and disgust at what he was saying. Some rose to argue, but he held up his hand, and said, "Hear me out, please."

They went back and forth, some getting upset, talking about ethics, threatening to leave. But he had them all won over by the end of the evening.

He had outdone himself this time. A genius was among them. He single-handedly would defeat Hitler, reverse the Jewish policy in Germany.

They voted to do it. But they seemed sad too.

"Where are you going?" Torres asked him as they were getting ready to leave and he sighed heavily.

Moro Giafferi turned back, looking as if he were weighed down with all the world's sorrow. "To make the boy revile me."

The moon was setting as Moro Giafferi's car took him to the entrance to the Fresnes prison.

It was the latest he had ever come. And Moro Giafferi was alone, Herschel saw—for the first time since their introduction. Now maybe—

"War may be declared soon," the man said with no introduction.

"Is that good for us?"

He sighed and shook his head. "No, my young friend—war is not good for anybody."

Herschel blushed. He had only been trying to make conversation.

"We who are charged with defending you had a meeting, and for some nearly a parting, this evening. But we have come to a decision. A necessary one.

"If we could acquit you any other way but this, we would." Moro Giafferi continued. "I'm not happy. I don't want to put you through it, but I've been thinking, and the French and the Germans have too. There's just no telling how the Nazis will react if you are acquitted of murder, Herschel. They might retaliate, start blaming Jews even more, attack France for setting you free, start more murdering. Do you understand?"

Herschel nodded.

"It does not mean that I will give up on you, son. But we must start over."

"Oh." Now was the moment to speak about Ernst.

"The truth will not do." He sounded so tragic that Herschel looked up.

"I have a plan; I think it will work and get you out.

You'll have to be brave." Moro Giafferi took a deep breath: "You must say—you must swear . . ."

Herschel held his breath. "You must say that vom Rath was not a stranger—that you knew him. You must say you lied about its being . . . for—"

"Lied?"

"It'll be the end of my professional career, and for all of us defending you, if you tell a soul. But we have no choice, you—I—to get the future we want, the truth will not do. You have to repudiate it."

"How?"

Moro Giafferi pointed at the table, where Herschel's journal lay. "Your diary." Herschel picked it up and was about to speak when the lawyer told him, "You must tell Judge Tesnieres that you and vom Rath—you should start calling him Ernst now—were familiar with each other."

Herschel jumped.

"Say," he cleared his throat, "that . . . he assaulted you—sexually, as a man would a woman."

He spun around.

"Or you were a prostitute and he was blackmailing you; or that you were blackmailing him to save your family!"

"But I—"

"Don't you see? In Germany they're torturing Jews—and blaming you."

The look in Herschel's eyes made him uneasy.

"I have sons too: I know how it must disgust a good

boy like you to think of those things—perverts are disgusting. But if we say that vom Rath was a dirty homosexual and that he raped you and that's why you shot him, it'll make a laughingstock of him, of Hitler, the whole country."

"No! That's not true!"

Moro Giafferi reached for Herschel, for his drawn-up shoulders, to massage them, but Herschel broke free. "Listen: Say he was a pervert and that he came at you—then you'd have had a reason to shoot. Homosexuals are sick! You'll go free!"

"But," Herschel croaked, "my diary—"

"You can say you were too ashamed to write such horrible things."

"I can't—in front of everyone, Solly! My family!"

"I understand," Moro Giafferi said gently. "But there's tens of thousands you can save if you stop giving the Nazis reasons for slaughtering Jews. You can tell your family later that you were lying. Just humble yourself now—tell them that you had sex with vom Rath for money—to save your family."

"But I didn't!"

Moro Giafferi squatted down and spoke earnestly to Herschel, who had slumped to his knees.

"You have no other choice. It's the only way out, believe me."

He sat still. "You will obey."

A minute passed and Herschel nodded, thinking, It's over. Everyone would laugh; they'd point and make obscene gestures from doorways. "Ernst!" he cried.

"Yes! Like that!"

Moro Giafferi released him. "You have to do it, son," he said. "Lie. Just like the Nazis do. Change your past, and then the future will change too."

He leaned down to Herschel. Hadn't he had a birthday recently? Wasn't he eighteen?

"It's never important who you are, boy. But what you can do, become, achieve."

He was at the door. "Believe me."

As the trial date was delayed and postponed and ultimatums passed in Europe, Moro Giafferi did not visit for weeks, haunted by the idea that he had somehow failed. Every now and then he acknowledged that he was curious about what the boy must be thinking. "Does he ever ask for me?" he inquired of the defense team.

They shook their heads.

"He doesn't ask for anything."

From the window of his cell Herschel continued to watch the world. He had seen fall become winter, the dreariest in years. Now, suddenly, the tips of trees reached for light, swaying as if they wanted to waltz, were obeying some unheard melody. He watched, waiting to be moved, by beauty, by a breeze. He held his hand out. He touched his wet cheek.

As summer blossomed, couples pressed hotel orchestras for one more dance. They lingered in the swooning air. Waiters brought one more serving. In September, the most golden in memory, Germany invaded Poland.

Denmark and the Netherlands fell the following spring. German tanks approached the border.

"France will never fall," Moro Giafferi told Herschel one evening.

But the Germans crossed into France on 13 May 1940.

By the end of the month Paris was threatened.

Herschel had been briefed. Told what would likely happen. And to be ready instantly.

So he was awake the night that his cell door opened.

It was a French soldier, thin, with a slight moustache, handsome. There was a noise in the hall, and the man darted back toward the door and looked out.

"It's now."

Herschel nodded but did nothing.

"Hurry up," the soldier said, throwing clothes at him. "You know what's expected." Herschel dressed, ran around for things to pack. He grabbed his diary.

"No. Leave it." (It would be discovered there within the week.)

The soldier opened the door and peered out.

"Make no sound. The Germans want you. No one must see." He motioned, and Herschel slipped through the dark hall to the metal stairs. He plunged down and, despite the fear, felt suddenly alive with the thrilling heaviness and weightlessness of what the drowning must feel. Outside, night was cool, the walls of buildings and trunks of the trees vivid, haloed in a glow of light; silence caressed the scene. Herschel wanted to stop, to touch the wall, breathe in. But someone grabbed him and yanked him into the shadows as lights swept the walls of the brick courtyard.

A car appeared.

He was thrust in and the shades pulled. In the distance he heard a vibration. Germans were approaching the city.

By noon the car had slowed, stuck in the traffic that caught all souls fleeing Paris. Germans were just beyond. Cars, handcarts, horses, and mules jammed the roads. All panicked as a plane flew low. The pamphlets fell as silently as snow. The car took off across a field.

They made it to Orléans by nightfall; strong arms opened the car door. No one spoke. Guards pushed him along an unlit interior hallway. Electric torches bobbed; voices urged, Vite! Vite!

But for a moment Herschel tasted the air and smelled trees. He looked around and said to the air, "I'm free."

He slept well, like a child who knows he is cared for. He was smiling when the French guard woke him in the gray light of false dawn. He thanked the man for the plate of dry bread and cheese.

In the vast courtyard groups of people sat in different chalked circles. Some were well dressed, with suitcases and antiques; others huddled together with no belongings. A man with a stick herded a flock of honking geese. When a guard motioned, Herschel stood and was led to an arched opening. People turned to see who the important personage could be.

But they saw only a boy with dark brooding eyes and olive skin.

The boy turned his eyes back on them. Behind him loomed a covered truck, its engine running, and, beyond it, green fields. The back doors of the truck opened and others reached for him. Then the door closed, plunging the back of the truck into near darkness. Several well-dressed men (in suits and shined shoes) urged him to the bench. At the back were crates and a large painting wrapped in burlap.

From the mesh window Herschel peered out, as the countryside flashed by, somnolent and green. Swaying hypnotically, he gave in to the scalding, baking heat.

For hours he slept and woke and looked at the greenery, hazed with heat and the chaff of wheat floating overhead. With a start and a jolt he woke with a ringing in his ears; all the men had looked up. Something dived lower. He could hear and feel it coming. The painting slid along the floor as the truck veered. One of the men reached for it.

"Vermeer," he said, but the truck hit a bump and the man hit his head on the low ceiling. Another bump and the doors opened, flinging Herschel out, like a soul rising. He flew up and the sky came at him. The world was upside down now—but only for a moment, for everything switched positions, and the earth came up to catch him. He fell to its soft yielding lap, and the truck fell away from under him.

Stunned, he could not breathe. People screamed, men hurtled forward, crawling over him.

The airplane dropped another bomb. The earth shuddered, convulsing like an animal—huge and trembling. Herschel could hear it groaning in fear. Dirt rose like hallelujahs and then fell in clumps all around him. He smelled gasoline.

"Run," a bleeding man screamed.

"They're coming!"

He started in the direction of the truck, but someone grabbed him. "The other way. This way, son. Run!"

After a while, Herschel slowed, falling farther and farther behind. He could not remember who he was exactly, what he should be doing. He just wanted to sit, be, think.

He slept that night with thousands of other refugees who lay out under the vast stars that seemed far away and uninvolved with them down here. With his ear to the ground, unable to sleep, he heard it again, deep within the earth, a groaning. Next to him was a Dutch family whose two daughters stayed up, eyes wide open, barely blinking.

When he woke, he could hardly breathe for the stitch in his side. Nearby, a group of refugees, silhouetted against the white sky, squatted on their heels, listening to a radio. The word of France's surrender drifted like smoke over the encampment. Unoccupied France was ordered to give over its political enemies.

All were urged to look. The list included the diplomat Ernst vom Rath's murderer, Herschel Grynszpan.

In the towns most windows were shuttered; some of those fleeing beat on the doors and windows, begging to be let in. But faces appeared only at upper windows — and they were frightened, white, pitying.

Herschel tried to catch the driver's eye as a car roared down the middle of the street, honking, scattering those in its way like sheep. He saw a little girl look from the car's back window. She waved. "Remember me. Tell them you saw Herschel Grynszpan."

The next day he passed the car, which was now a burned-out shell on the side of the road. Leading from it were papers, a doll, and an opened suitcase, a scattering of belongings.

That afternoon he came upon a long mansard-roofed building with palms in pots on either side of a curling staircase. Herschel went up the steps and peered into the darkness.

A man was eating his meal on a table in the space created by two intersecting hallways. He was sunken-mouthed, grizzled.

"I need to be seen," Herschel told him. "I have secrets I must tell somebody."

The man smiled and nodded.

"I'm from Paris! I was being taken to safety—but a plane hit us. The Germans—"

"The mayor's office is over there," the man said, inclining his head.

Herschel ran through the open door.

And out.

"But it's empty!"

"Yes, sir. No one here."

Herschel stamped his feet—and there was an odd echo because the hallway was a tunnel that ran the whole length of the building. Through it he saw, as if looking through the tube of a telescope, the end of the row of trees and road. He saw others in the dusty distance.

On the road he caught up with a group of several families and a few lone men; when he spoke, they became quiet.

"German," he heard them whispering.

He let them pass. He felt safer alone. Birds circled and soared above, victors of the fields. To anyone watching he must have looked like a scarecrow. He ate radishes, potatoes, raw green weeds. And when he looked up from retching, a brown-eyed yellow dog with a thick wagging tail was watching him curiously, kindly.

The sun rose meaninglessly morning after morning, arching like a shell hurled over the earth; as it descended, it gilded the evening's shimmering fields. Bombs fell at night to the north, ecstatic bright flashes like lightning. Never was life more beautiful or precious, so worth living. After a week of hiding in ditches, of sleep snatched in barns and fields, he came upon a city with a river and red brick buildings.

People turned away from him, as if from the truth.

"I've escaped," he babbled, rushing into the police station. "Help me. I'm from Paris; I'm important to the state; there'll be a reward. Ask, call Paris—they'll come for me."

Silently and wide-eyed the somber men looked at him.

"But the Germans are in Paris. Vichy is the capital now."

"What do you mean?"

"The treaty," a gendarme prompted. "With Germany."

"No—you don't understand! Call. There's a reward. You'll see."

There was.

On 4 July 1940 Herschel Grynszpan was turned over by Vichy France and flown to Berlin. Those who turned him in were rewarded handsomely.

Records reveal that the Germans imprisoned Herschel Grynszpan outside Berlin in the part of the Sachsenhausen concentration camp reserved for dignitaries. It was rumored among the guards that an ambassador and a foreign secretary were held there.

"You must be important," an inmate, a tall skinny man with a patchy beard, told Herschel early one dark morning. "They have special plans for you." But the man was caught talking to him and marched away at gunpoint, before Herschel could ask him anything.

The boy was kept in a cell by himself after that. Every now and then a man in civilian clothes from Berlin would come and just look at him. Someone came and took photographs; then a tailor came and measured him.

That made him think of Uncle Abraham. And it made Herschel cold, wondering what had happened to him and Aunt Chawa. And if his family back in Poland was surviving.

After months of waiting, the head of the camp came and told him he could make himself useful to the Reich while they waited for his disposition. Herschel was made an orderly to a half-dozen guards of the prison.

But two were reassigned. So soon only four guards shared a room with bunk beds.

Herschel came when they rang; he shined the shoes that they left out for him in the morning. And he eavesdropped on what they said of him.

"He's so small," the guard with the dark moustache weighed in. "How can he be important?"

The other, with a scar on his cheek, grunted and motioned Herschel over, "Come here, baby."

He kissed him.

Another fellow, tall and colorless, laughed.

Herschel tried to join in, to be friendly, tried to start conversations when he brought their shaving water and pressed clothes.

But he could not.

And they changed after a while, held back. It was if they could see something horrible looming over his shoulder that he could not. They seemed to know what was being planned for him.

"Save me," he wanted to scream.

But he knew, and it made him feel guilty, that he had it easy.

Prisoners, not special ones like him, were penned in by the hundreds. They seemed more like animals in herds than people with feelings and dreams. He watched them and tried but could not catch a sense of their personalities or look them in their eyes. For if he thought about what they were going through, it would tear him apart, make him crazy. The prisoners in the ordinary part of the camp were awakened and taken out before dawn every morning to work in clay pits to make bricks, but fewer returned in the evening.

They suffered, not he.

He had his own room. If the guards wanted him, they pulled a string; in his cell a bell at the top of the wall rang and he went running. Every time he entered the door of the barracks, Herschel paused and listened.

After a while they stopped talking when he came into the room. Some Jew, the rumors went, would be removed soon; he would be taken to Berlin for a great trial where all would see how his race had weakened the fabric of Germany.

"What's that mean to us?" the tall colorless one asked. And the fellow in the bunk below, who was short and stocky and had dirty underpants, answered, "We'll get a new orderly."

Herschel heard laughing.

"Hey, baby boy," the tall one cried when he came in; all asked to have their pictures taken with him. They sent them home with notes on the back. This was the Jew who had murdered vom Rath and started the war between France and Germany.

The next week a team arrived from the Reich propaganda ministry, under Herr Doktor Goebbels. They needed information from him.

"Certainly," Herschel agreed.

They began pleasantly, asking questions like reporters. How much had he been paid? Who, they asked, had recruited him to kill vom Rath and bring on war? Who did he report to? Paris's chief rabbi? How many were in the conspiracy?

When he told them that it was not so and that he had gone to the embassy to plead and make a statement about his family, they looked bored and rolled their eyes. When he stopped, they handed him a sheet. "Sign a confession and you'll go free."

Herschel read it but then put the paper down. "I'll do it. But only if you release my family."

They shook their heads and said they did not know where they were.

Then he would not sign. He consoled himself by thinking that someday people might remember Herschel Grynszpan for standing up against the greatest evil. Picturing it made him cry, thinking of his resistance and all the madness and cruelty.

After a week the team from Berlin left, and he went back to the routine. Soon, he could not say how long after, a new group of men came. They were younger and mean, handsome, all blond and lean. They did not ask now but screamed when he did not answer. He understood this, was almost happy with it, as if finally they were using a language he could speak.

One man took delight in torturing him. Jagusch had thin lips and ice-cold green eyes; he was pale, but his cheeks and ears got red as he screamed. He'd come into Herschel's room and shout in the middle of the night; he'd fling off the covers and grab Herschel out of bed. Herschel grimaced as the man took him by the hair and pulled his head back, almost gagging.

Then he let his head down and threw him to the floor and kicked him. A boot was in front of his face. Herschel licked it.

"Tell me what you know," the man said, disgusted, drawing away.

"I will. I want to make a statement," he gasped as the man started to bounce his truncheon on his neck.

Jagusch turned polite and stopped. "Someone will come from Berlin right away."

"But I want you."

So handsome officer Jagusch, dashing and blond, took the statement down. It meant a promotion, surely.

From the Confession of Herschel Grynszpan
Reich Main Security Prison
January 1942

One night in the summer of 1938 I was walking in Paris by the river. Crying. A man stopped and asked why I was so sad. He worked in the embassy. If I did what he wanted, he would help with a visa, he said, help me with my family.

All for just getting in the car with him. So I did. We went to a hotel. He offered me money.

I only went with vom Rath because he could get my family out. I saw him again and again — and he made me do perversions. I hated him. It was disgusting.

When I got postcards from my family saying they had been deported, I bought a gun. If he did not do what I demanded, I'd see the ambassador. My lawyer in France — Vincent de Moro Giafferi — knows this too. Harm me and he'll tell everything.

— Herschel Feibel Grynszpan

Joseph Goebbels was told right away of the Jew's confession. He could not tell a soul. Only his diary.

24 January 1942. The murder trial of the Jew Grynszpan is being held up. He confessed and made up an insolent lie that he and vom Rath were carrying on a homosexual relationship. That is, of course, shameless but cleverly thought out; if brought to light in the trial, it would ruin everything.

Probably that Corsican lawyer of his, he must be Jewish too, had dreamed it up. Think of how the soldiers and the men running the camps would react. The very idea — Grynszpan and vom Rath? A German and a Jew; two men, enemies.

The Führer could not know of such disgusting things; without a doubt, it would make him very angry. On all fronts, at home and abroad, all had to go smoothly.

For a few weeks Herschel had peace. No one came from Berlin. He lay on his bed and tucked his knees up as close to his chin as he could get them. It made him feel like someone was cradling him.

Maybe Moro Giafferi was right. Maybe this would slow down the killing.

But somehow the guards got wind; they came for him and pushed him into closets and pointed at their swelling trousers.

"Jew whore," they shouted.

"No, please." He fought and clawed and screamed.

When he came to in the mornings, he did not get out of bed. He clung to himself, held on to his long striped sleeves as he shivered and watched the bodies pass to and from the brick pit, as dawn reddened the sky.

They were wretches, stick creatures that would not make it back in the evening. He watched one swaying in line on the way to the pit. He was so thin that Herschel did not understand how the man could stay alive. Herschel watched with disbelief, disgust, and pity. Give up! he wanted to scream at the creature as it tottered along. Then maybe he could take his eyes off it. Give in.

Many did; they ran for the electrified fences and screamed as they writhed and smoked and slowly stopped when the current was turned off. Others just fell. The guards came up. If the prisoner did not respond, a gun butt would put him out of his suffering.

200

Herschel watched the thin coughing creature list and spin. He fell and lay with red mouth open, wan eyes staring. It made Herschel angry; he was horrified to watch hope and happiness light the creature's face as it smiled, like a candle in a skull, as it saw another prisoner approach. The creature on the ground reached.

And something moved in Herschel. He felt a memory stir, was aware of a subtle shift within. It could not be, and if it was, it did not mean anything, yet Herschel watched excitedly. The man who stepped out of line to help the fallen creature—something in him was riveting and alive. He bent to the pathetic thing. It hurt to watch the man put his arms out, enfold, and lift the skeleton; the thing's mouth opened in a rictus. A skeletal finger came up and the other man's lips came down to him.

Herschel grasped the windowsill. "At the El Dorado in Paris! I saw them!"

It made him mad; it made him sing; it made him think of Ernst in angst, anger, and envy. He understood how he could survive, how important he could be.

He called for Officer Jagusch immediately.

From the Confessions of Herschel Grynszpan
Reich Main Security Prison
Final entry

I lied in my last confession.

Ernst vom Rath loved me.

When my family was deported, I went to the embassy. The ambassador was out; I was told I would be taken to the highest officer on duty.

It was Ernst. I was going to kill myself. I had

the gun in my mouth and was going to die, but Ernst wouldn't let me. He loved me.

I loved him, too.

I sign this confession willingly.

—Herschel Feibel Grynszpan

Now they were known, and, like light from dead stars, would come down through the years. The dark would disappear.

The propaganda minister balled up the confession. He paced the floor, hitting his forehead with the flat of his hand. He went to his desk and reached for his diary.

> *24 March 1942. I am having a terrible time, trying to get all in order for the Grynszpan trial. The Jew had claimed until just now that he never even knew the counselor of legation, vom Rath, whom he shot. Now he's changed his story, and there's surfaced bits of evidence to support the possibility of relations between Grynszpan and vom Rath.*

Bitterly, he retrieved the file and saw the testimony of the women from the apartment building at 23 Richard Lenoir; the Hotel Istanbul clerk; the photographs of a carving of initials on a windowsill.

He'd kill the witnesses, destroy the window, shred Herschel's confession personally.

But still, a German and Jew.

Disgusting.

Afterword

The last time anyone saw Herschel Grynszpan in the Sachsenhausen Concentration Camp was September 1942. In the middle of the night, a car came for him.

Months later Adolf Hitler and Joseph Goebbels were still corresponding about him. Goebbels had confessed the possibility of an intimate relationship between vom Rath and Grynszpan. And the Führer, as expected, was angry. For it meant the big show trial had to wait. Grynszpan was too risky, could ruin everything.

While they waited, the war turned. The Russian front proved disastrous. The Allies landed at Normandy. Troops eventually ringed Berlin. Hitler and Goebbels committed suicide within a few feet of each other in the Reich chancellery building.

Their papers were on fire when the Russians marched in. Over the years many documents relating to the case of Herschel Grynszpan were found—including Goebbels's diary in which he expressed his fears that the relationship of Ernst vom Rath and Herschel Grynszpan would be found out.

That entry (and others) are included in these pages. Other surviving documents are used as well: the press release from the physicians whom Hitler sent to Paris, Joseph Goebbels's speech in Munich the night before Kristallnacht, the radio address of Dorothy Thompson, and the postcards from the Grynszpan family. All are copied (some in translation and paraphrase) from the historical record.

The story of young Grynszpan's life (and/or Kristallnacht) can be traced in these sources:

Marino, Andy. *Herschel: The Boy Who Started World War II*. Boston: Faber and Faber, 1995.

Read, Anthony, and David Fisher. *Kristallnacht: Unleashing the Holocaust*. London: Michael Joseph, 1989.

Schwab, Gerald. *The Day the Holocaust Began: The Odyssey of Herschel Grynszpan*. New York: Praeger, 1990.

Thalman, Rita, and Emmanuel Feinermann. *Crystal Night: 9–10 November 1938*. Trans. Gilles Cremonesi. London: Thames and Hudson, 1974. Originally published as *La Nuit de Cristal: 9–10 Novembre 1938*. Paris: Editions Robert Laffont, 1972.

Nearly all base their information about Herschel, including the known extracts from his diary, on Dr. Alain Cuenot's "The Herschel Grynszpan Case," an unpublished narrative in French, an English translation of which is in the Library of Congress.

Many of these works openly affirm Herschel's declaration that he was gay and that he and Ernst were in a relationship, but most historians try to explain it away, as if labeling Herschel as gay insults him and makes him less of an "innocent" victim. And those who believe Herschel assume that any such relationship between a Jew and a German had to be tawdry. I began to write this story to restore Herschel to history as a gay man—and to give him the possibility of having had some happiness. I have tried to stay as true to the actual historical events as possible, but I have compressed time and changed the family's early history. I have created some relationships wholly out of my imagination. But Herschel himself is pretty much as I found him—puzzling, annoying, contradictory, adolescent, and tragic.

In the early 1950s a minor Nazi official named Solitkow, intrigued by the story, created a furor by publishing an article about Herschel and Ernst's relationship. (Some 1930s diaries describing them as gay have come to light since then, while a few historians theorize that the idea was planted in Herschel's head by his attorney, Moro Giafferi.) Guenther, the sole surviving member of the vom Rath family, was so upset by the allegations in the article that he took legal action. The charge that Guenther lodged against Solitkow was "libeling the deceased."

The trial drew much attention, and many packed the galleries. Some stated that Herschel Grynszpan himself was among those attending. (All his family survived the war, except Uncle Abraham, who was murdered in Auschwitz, and Berta, who died in Russia where the family took refuge. Sendel would later testify at Adolph Eichmann's trial in Jerusalem, describing their expulsion from Germany to Poland.) The judge in the Solitkow case demanded Herschel Grynszpan, if alive, to appear.

The press descended to cover this sensational event, but Herschel did not turn up. (If he was alive, he still could have been tried for the murder of vom Rath; even if he had been acquitted, he could then have been imprisoned for his homosexuality.) The jury ordered punishment for Solitkow, who had never been punished for his Nazi activities.

Although rumors persisted that Herschel was living in Paris, New York, or Tel Aviv, and although his brother advertised for him for years, Herschel Grynszpan never reappeared.

To bring his family peace, and to stop the rumors, the German government granted him a death date; this, it was hoped, would bring closure and supply an ending to his story.

But it has not. Herschel, the subject of an oratorio, an opera, a television documentary, and an international search, still mystifies and intrigues. There are so many theories about this adolescent with hauntingly dark eyes whose life was so sad and so unsettling.

DATE DUE

GAYLORD No. 2333   PRINTED IN U.S.A.